Acknowledgments and Thanks

Many thanks to my God and my family for support and love beyond measure.

THE COVID CHRONICLES

BOOK 2

SURVIVING THE APOCALYPSE

Skip Coryell

Published by White Feather Press. (www.whitefeatherpress. com)

ISBN 978-1-61808-195-7
Exterior cover photo ©shutterstock.com/Andrii Vodolazhskyi
Printed in the United States of America

White Feather Press

Reaffirming Faith in God, Family, and Country!

Books by Skip Coryell

We Hold These Truths
Bond of Unseen Blood
Church and State
Blood in the Streets
Laughter and Tears
RKBA: Defending the Right to Keep and Bear Arms
Stalking Natalie
The God Virus
The Shadow Militia
The Saracen Tide
The Blind Man's Rage
Civilian Combat - The Concealed Carry Book
Jackpine Strong
Concealed Carry for Christians
The Covid Chronicles: Surviving the Upgrade
The Covid Chronicles: Surviving the Apocalypse

From the author

April 23rd, 2020

When I first started writing *The Covid Chronicles*, I didn't know for sure if there would be a second book. I wanted to leave it open for that, but a writer never knows how his work will be accepted until he throws it out to the world. It's a vulnerable thing, to show the world what you're thinking. But there has been sufficient interest and appreciation for the book to merit a second, so here I go again. To be sure, reviews were mixed. In fact, I was criticized by some people for writing about the Covid pandemic. I was told it shouldn't be done, that it was in poor taste. Of course, that's a political concern, and this book is fairly devoid of politics. That's one of the things about the apocalypse. There are no republicans or democrats; we're just all people, trying to survive. All our flavors are gone.

To be sure, I was greatly disappointed when Amazon first refused to offer the book on its website, but, after time had passed and common sense prevailed, it was listed for sale there.

Some of you may notice that this story is more overtly "Christian" than my other novels. This isn't because I'm preaching or trying to convert you to my way of thinking ... it's just me being me. The older I get, the more I realize that my time here is limited, and, if there's anything I want to say, anything the world needs to hear, then I'd best get on with it while I still can. Mortality will do that to an aging man.

The characters in this story are special to me; they are personal; they embody the values and hopes and dreams of everything that is important to me. Mag is a younger me, much younger. The other characters are composites or altered versions of people in my life whom I love. One thing I've learned in life is this: when you find someone who loves you, someone loyal, someone brave, then it's a good idea to hold on tight and keep them in your life.

This novel, more than any of the others, required my active imagination, simply because no one living has ever experienced the apocalypse, or the end of the world as we know it. So I constantly caught myself thinking while writing ... what would it be like without traffic, without electricity, without the ability to travel, without 5,000 friends on FaceBook, without communication to the outside world. And the answers to those questions are the pages of this book.

It's a harder world, less forgiving, primitive, perhaps even barbaric in some ways but ... the important things shine through. In a primitive world, all the superfluous, extraneous garbage is stripped away, and all that is left is what's important in life. What is that for me? My belief in God; my love for my family; the singing of the crickets while watching the sun go down on a summer night.

My hope is that my readers will also be tempted to examine themselves anew, to truly study life and decide what's most important to you. Once you figure that out; it's just a matter of living life to its fullest, in accordance with everything you believe and all you hold dear. I hope you enjoy the story.

– Skip Coryell

What has gone before...

In book one of this series, *The Covid Chronicles: Surviving the Upgrade*, Mag Jacobs, an aspiring author found himself trapped in Michigan's upper peninsula at the onset of the world's deadliest pandemic to date. Covid-19.1, "The Upgrade" as it is being called, has a comunicability rate of 95 percent. Nine out of ten who contract this disease will die.

Mag's efforts to make it home backfire, and he finds himself floating helplessly in the middle of Lake Michigan with no apparent means to make landfall. It is revealed that Covid-19.1 is a bioweapon launched by the Chinese government, and the American president unleashes an all-out conventional weapons attack to prevent them from invading the American homeland. But the war quickly escalates into a nuclear stand-off where cities all over the globe are destroyed by nuclear missiles.

Finally, Mag makes it back to his wife and three kids just in time for the end of the world as we know it. Welcome home, Mag!

And thus, the story begins where it left off. I am proud to give you ... *The Covid Chronicles: Surviving the Apocalypse*!

For Sara, my dear wife,
whom I love and fight for.

And to my children.

> *"That is why it was called Babel—because there the Lord confused the language of the whole world. From there the Lord scattered them over the face of the whole earth."*
>
> *Genesis 11:9 (NIV)*

CHAPTER I

<u>Hickory Flats, MI - Jacobs Family Home</u>

MICHAEL HAD THE LAST WATCH of the night. He sat in the porch swing, listening to the sounds of early morning: the wings of an owl as it made its way back to roost; two raccoons fighting in the distant woods; and then the sounds of robins, finches and sparrows as they began their day, flitting to and fro from branch to branch in their never-ending quest for seeds and bugs and worms.

Michael enjoyed this time of day, the solitude, the great awakening, the changing of nature's guard as all the animals took their rightful place, transitioning from night to day. Slowly, the blackness of the night gave way to gray, and then a growing light as the sun began to rise in the east.

In the quickening bustle of the dawn, the young man thought about his future. Everything had changed. A week ago he'd been set on a career in the military, going to

1

college, maybe ROTC and then becoming an officer. But that wouldn't happen now; more than that ... it *couldn't* happen now. So many options and opportunities ... gone.

He thought about his friends, the ones who weren't answering his text messages or phone calls, and he wondered ... *are they all dead*? And what about the four men he'd killed a few days ago. The mechanics of it had been so easy. He'd just snuck up in the tall grass, like he'd done so many times before with Cypress while playing air soft wars; then he'd pulled the pin and tossed it up beside the truck. He still remembered the look of surprise on one man's face as he watched the round, fragmentation grenade bounce toward him and then roll to a stop between his legs. His eyes had gotten big, and then Michael had ducked his head down behind the bank for protection. The explosion had been so large, so deafening, and the smells had surprised him. Before then he hadn't realized that death had a smell ... but it did. And Michael would never forget it, no matter how much he wanted to.

He heard the screen door open up and glanced over in time to see his mother. She came over and sat down beside him.

"You're up early."

She nodded and put her arm around her son and started to scratch his neck. The Jacobs family had always been free with physical affection for one another.

"I couldn't sleep, son. You know how I am. When I wake up, no matter what time it is, I just can't get back to sleep again. I learned a long time ago just to get up and do something useful, because I'm not getting back to sleep."

There was enough light now to see all the way to the road. "Dad's the same way, right?"

Karen nodded. "Yep. He's always been like that. It's a

wonder either one of us gets any sleep at all."

And then she looked at him, trying to decipher what was going on inside his head. "What ya thinking, son?"

Michael didn't want to answer her. He felt a certain amount of shame in what he'd done, at the killing of four men. Finally he answered her.

"I killed those men, Mom."

Her muscles tensed up, and Karen didn't answer right away. At first she didn't know what to say, but gradually, it came to her.

"Your dad told me you'd be struggling with that. He's having a bit of a hard time with the men he killed as well."

"Really?" Michael looked over at her.

"Yeah. So is your Uncle Johnny."

A slight breeze kicked up, but died back down as quickly as it had started.

"What did Dad say about it?"

Karen was amazed at men, how they seldom talked openly about their feelings, especially to one another. If she'd killed a man she wouldn't be able to keep her mouth shut about it. But these Jacobs men ... they just suffered quietly.

"He said it was natural to feel bad about killing some-one. We're not supposed to like it or want to do it, no mat-ter what the circumstances are. He said it was the context of the killing that mattered most."

Michael's young brow furrowed in deep thought. "Context? What did he mean by that?"

She changed the subject for just a moment. "Isn't it odd how we can't hear the traffic from US 131 anymore?"

Michael didn't answer. She continued on. "Sometimes it's less important what you did, and more important why you did it." She gazed out across the lawn and the farmer's cornfield beyond the road, all the way out to the highway that she couldn't see. "So, why did you kill those men, son?"

Michael looked down at the AR-15 in his hands. He clenched it tightly, but wanted to throw it off to the side and never pick it up again.

"Because they were trying to kill Dad and Uncle Johnny."

Karen nodded her head. "And what would have happened if you and Buzz hadn't intervened?"

Her son's eyes moistened over. The words came out hard for him. "Then ... Dad would have died."

"Yes, that's probably true." She squeezed his neck in quiet reassurance. "You did the right thing, Michael. You saved your dad's life from bad men who were trying to kill him. It's as simple as that. Don't try to over-think this thing."

Michael blinked away the tears before they could fully form and run down his cheeks. "What would you have done, Mom?"

Karen hesitated while she thought about it. When she answered it was with a firm and convincing conviction. "Anyone who tries to hurt my family has to die. That's just the way it is now." And then she added. "But I guess it's always been that way; it just seems more important and real to me now."

Oddly enough, Michael felt comforted by his mother's violent proclamation. Neither of them said anything else. They just sat there quietly, soaking in the peace of the morning. Finally, Karen leaned over and kissed her son on the cheek before getting up.

"I'm gonna make breakfast. I'll call when it's ready, son." The door slammed softly behind her, and Michael stared out into the dawn, looking for threats, and contemplating her wisdom.

THE BEDROOM WINDOW WAS OPEN JUST A CRACK, SO Mag awakened to the sound of birds. He lay there for several minutes, not wanting to get up. Quite frankly, he didn't want to be in the waking world. He wanted sleep ... unconsciousness, beautiful, blissful ignorance and incoherence. In short, Mag was hesitant to deal with the new day; perhaps, didn't even know how to take it on. His mind started to whirl now, and he knew sleep would never return to him.

So many questions ... so few answers.

Mag threw off the sheet and blanket and sat up on the bed. He was in his underwear and a t-shirt, looking down at his left foot and the giant scab that had formed between his first and second toes. It was healing nicely. He moved his left shoulder back and forth, then pulled the shirt up and looked at the bandage. There was no blood soaked through and less soreness than yesterday.

Coffee. He needed coffee.

Mag stood slowly and gingerly put weight on his sprained ankle. It was better today. He longed for the days of his youth when the only time he hurt was when he was injured or had exercised too much. Now he was sore just for waking up. And then he wondered, *Buzz is 67 years old, it must be worse for him.* He made a mental note to ask him about it.

As Mag walked over to the shower, he undressed and thought about his day. Things were so different now. He didn't have to write books. In fact, as far as he knew, there was no one left in the world to read them, even if he could figure out a way to get them printed. It was the same for his concealed carry classes. His family all carried guns throughout the day, but no one bothered to conceal anymore. What was the point? There was no one out there to see the guns anyway. And there was no one to take his concealed carry classes. And then he thought to himself *How many people are left in the world?* They hadn't seen anyone on the road in two days. The last people they'd seen, they'd had to kill in self-defense.

And then a silver lining occurred to him. *I don't need to earn money anymore. The bank is toast. I own my house now.*

After his shower, he dressed and strapped on his Glock 19 Guttersnipe pistol. Then he went to the kitchen. The others were already sitting at the table and Karen and Katy were bringing the food. He looked up at the clock. It was already after 8AM.

"Anyone seen my brother, yet?"

"No way, Dad. I think he's still sleeping."

And then he walked over to the coffee maker and poured himself a cup. "Thanks for making coffee, dear." And he gave his wife a kiss. Eventually, they were all seated at the table.

"Katy, will you say grace this morning?"

Katy smiled. She always liked it when her father chose her for meal-time prayers. She clasped her small hands and bowed her head.

"Dear Jesus. This is a really good day. Thanks for bringing Daddy home. Bless this food to our bodies. Please help my friends from church not to die of the virus. Amen."

Everyone else echoed, "Amen." Then Karen and Mag glanced at each other and made eye contact. And that's when Mag made the decision to try and find out who else was left alive out there.

"Michael, did you see anyone or hear anything on watch this morning?"

Michael spooned a heap full of scrambled eggs into his mouth and chewed before answering. "Nothin, Dad. It was all quiet on the western front."

"What about you, Karen?"

She sipped her coffee. "I didn't hear anything except animals. It was a pretty quiet night."

"Has anyone seen any planes in the last few days?"

None of them had.

"What about trains? The tracks that run between Kalamazoo and Grand Rapids are only 2 miles away."

Cypress was the first to speak. "I heard one day before yesterday."

Katy chimed in as well. "Me too, Dad."

Just then Johnny came into the house from the pole barn. "Morning everyone."

He walked over and got some coffee, then came and sat down with the rest of the family.

"So what's going on today?"

Karen looked up from her eggs. "We're trying to figure out if anyone else is still alive out there in the world. No one's heard or seen any cars or planes in over two days now."

He sipped his coffee. "Yeah, it was kinda weird last night on watch. No traffic from the highway, no planes flying over. Not even military flights. It's unusual."

Mag wondered in the privacy of his own mind if that many people could actually be dead. But his brother voiced his fears.

"But then again, we had nuclear missiles exploding all over the place not to mention violence in the streets."

He looked at his brother and smiled at that one. "You and I saw that one first hand on our way home. And we have no idea how many people died from the virus. For all we know, we're the last people on the planet."

"But Mary's okay, isn't she, Dad?" Mary was Katy's 9-year-old best friend from church. They hadn't been able to get through to them with their cell phones for 2 days now. They lived just a few miles away. Mag responded before his brother could say anything.

"I'm sure Mary's okay, honey. We'll try to call her again today, and if that doesn't work, I'll drive over in a few more days just to make sure they don't need anything."

Katy smiled at that and went back to eating her breakfast.

"I think we need to find out more information, so I was thinking I'd visit the colonel this morning."

Cypress interrupted his father. "Good idea, Dad. I'm getting nothing on my ham radio, but our range is pretty limited. But the colonel's got short wave, and with the mega-antennae he's got, on high ground, I know he reaches all over the world, especially when he picks up some skip in the early morning and just after sundown."

Mag nodded. "Honey, can you do without me for a few hours?"

Karen smiled. "If I don't die from a broken heart, I should be fine." He smiled back at her and sipped his coffee. It was already cooling off.

"So what are you doing, today, honey?"

Karen looked over at Katy when she answered him. "Katy and I are going to update the inventory of all our supplies. It'll probably take all day, but I think we need to know what we have so we can start rationing things."

"Great idea, sweetheart." And then he grinned widely at her. "God certainly smiled on me when I married you."

Cypress was quick to add, "That's right, Dad. You married up that's for sure."

Mag didn't know how to take that, so he let the comment pass. Karen smiled discreetly and winked at him. Mag finished up his breakfast and was the first to get up from the table.

"I'm heading to see Buzz now." And then, as an afterthought, he glanced back over his shoulder. "Are the cell phones still working?"

Michael laughed out loud. "Mine is, but yours is toast, Dad. You dropped it in Lake Michigan."

He frowned."Yeah, I remember." And then he turned to Karen. "Honey, just call Buzz on his cell if you need me for anything."

"Will do, sweetheart." He kissed her cheek on the way out and got a big hug from Katy as well. And then he was out the door.

GUNS AND THE APOCALYPSE

During times of complete societal breakdown, ownership of a firearm will be just as important as food and water. Think of it this way: You can go without food for about 2 weeks. You can go without water for 3 days. But how long will you live without a gun when someone is trying to kill you? Not very long. Maybe 5 seconds.

Regardless of your political views or moral beliefs, during the apocalypse, we become a lawless society. There is no central dispatch. You can't just call 911 for help. You've probably heard the phrase "When seconds count, the police are just minutes away." But after societal collapse, the police are home protecting their family - they are an infinity away.

In my opinion, it's never been a good idea to outsource your own personal protection. During the apocalypse, who are you going to hire to protect you? You will have to learn how to provide for your own defense if you are going to survive.

FIREARMS TRAINING

So many of my concealed carry students take my class because they want to "feel" safe. But I'm here to tell you that "feeling" safe isn't the same as "being" safe." Of course, safety itself has always been an illusion. Since the Fall of Man, the world has always been dangerous. Don't believe me? Ask Cain and Abel.

Here are some great places to get started on firearms training:

My own company, Midwest Tactical Training, www.mwtac.com (Michigan)

Frontsight Training Academy, (Nevada) www.frontsight.com

Rob Pincus, ICE Training Inc. www.icetraining.us (Nationwide)

Massad Ayoob, Massad Ayoob Group www.massadayoob.com (Nationwide)

Dave Spaulding, Handgun Combatives, Inc www.handguncombatives.com (Nationwide)

Midwest Training Group (Idaho & Iowa) www.midwesttraininggroup.net

> *"Remember those earlier days after you had received the light, when you endured in a great conflict full of suffering."*
>
> *Hebrews 10:32 (NIV)*

CHAPTER 2

Colonel Buzz Command Center

MAG ASKED **K**AREN TO SEND Buzz a text message saying that he was on his way over to see him; not to be polite, but to make sure the colonel didn't shoot him. Buzz was a dangerous man, and the last person Mag wanted to startle, especially after the apocalypse.

Just as he was about to knock on the door, it opened up and Buzz greeted him.

"Morning, Mag. Follow me and we'll head on down to the command post. I don't like leaving it alone for fear I might miss something important."

Once down inside the command center, Mag felt like he'd transported back in time and he was in the Marines again. There were more radios than he could shake a stick at and all were receiving at various volumes. Mag didn't waste any time.

"Buzz, I need to know what's going on in the world so

I can prepare my family."

The colonel was standing in front of his short wave base station. He turned the CB and the Ham radio off so he could hear better.

"This guy is from St. Louis, so that means Missouri probably didn't get nuked. I can tell as much by the silence as well as by the radio chatter."

Mag moved closer. "So who is silent?"

Buzz didn't answer. He just pointed up at the map on the wall to his right. Mag walked over and looked at the paper map, covered with acetate film and colored push pins. He was surprised to see so many.

"All these cities got nuked?"

Buzz nodded. "Sixteen in all."

Mag scanned the map and tried to memorize the names of the cities. He started on the west coast and worked his way east.

The west coast had been hit hard: San Diego, Los Angeles, San Francisco and Seattle. And then Colorado Springs and Omaha in the heartland. Texas was clobbered in Dallas and Houston and then neighboring New Orleans. The upper Midwest seemed to get off easy with only two nukes, one in Chicago and another in Cincinnati. Florida got off easy with only Miami at its southern tip being destroyed. Just to the north in Georgia, Atlanta and the CDC had taken a big hit. Of course, the mid-Atlantic states were devastated by big hits in Washington DC, New York City and Philadelphia.

Mag shook his head from side to side. "There must've been millions that died in the attacks."

Buzz turned down the radio so they could talk. Then he sat down on the padded stool behind him and motioned for Mag to do the same.

"Tens of millions, actually. You can look at it that way, or you can take the attitude that 90 percent of them were going to die anyway."

Mag gave him a funny look. It wasn't like Buzz to be so callus. The colonel saw his confused look.

"I'm talking about the bio-attack. Everything that I'm hearing on the short wave tells me this virus has a 90-plus percent mortality rate." He shrugged. Let's face it, most of the city folks were going to die anyway. The nukes just made it quick and painless for them."

Mag needed more time to think about that one. "You got some coffee, colonel?"

Buzz nodded his head over at the coffee pot and mugs. "Help yerself, non-com."

Mag smiled. The man was so military. Mag poured his coffee and sat back down.

"What makes you think it was a bio-attack?"

The colonel took a sip of his coffee. It was cold again, but he didn't seem to notice.

"I've been monitoring government frequencies. They talk about it even though they shouldn't. It's a human thing, I guess. When you feel alone and cut off, you tend to talk about the things that scare you."

"What else can you tell me?

"It was the Chinese without a doubt. Somehow the US found out about it and launched a conventional attack on China. All their seaports and navy bases for starters. China retaliated by sinking some of our subs and aircraft carriers. It was a bloodbath at sea."

Buzz pointed to his Go Army mug. "Freshen that up will ya, sergeant."

Mag didn't hesitate. He respected Buzz and wanted to know more. And then he smiled to himself and thought.

Once an officer, always an officer.

"I'm not sure how the Ruskies got involved. Somehow, somewhere, somebody made a mistake, pushed the wrong button, we'll probably never know for sure everything that happened. But ... once they started launching it was a free for all. A real cluster."

He blew the steam off his fresh coffee mug and took a sip. "Of course they could've decided on their own to get involved. You know, opportunity to dominate the world and all in the midst of all the chaos. But the bottom line is China and Russia got nuked just as hard as we did, maybe worse." Buzz set his coffee mug down on the bench top. "Pakistan and India nuked each other just out of spite I spose."

Mag glanced over at the map again and shook his head sadly. "I wonder how many died this past week."

Buzz laughed out loud. "It would be easier to count how many lived."

Mag raised one eyebrow in surprise. "That many?"

Buzz looked over at the map and nodded. "Yeah, without a doubt. Nukes are limited to an explosion and some fallout, but Covid 19.1 isn't limited by borders or wind direction or any of that. It spreads from host to host and coast to coast. Even without the nuclear war, 90 percent of the population would have died."

Mag squirmed on the padded stool. He sat there stunned, unable to respond. The colonel saw this and gave him a second to recover as he took a sip of his coffee. And then Mag finally asked.

"Buzz, why am I not dead? I was in that house on the lakeshore with the dead family. I was on my book tour the week before this all went down meeting and talking to hundreds of people. If anybody should be infected it should be me."

Buzz nodded. "True." He glanced down at his short wave radio, eager to get back to it. "All I can tell you is the theories that have been going back and forth on the air waves."

Mag leaned in closer, took a sip and waited.

"Most of the people talking are saying that the survivors fall into one of two camps: People who didn't get the first wave of the virus, and those who never leave their house."

Mag thought for a moment. "How are people supposed to know whether or not they got the first wave? Most people were never tested for it, and 80 percent who did get it didn't have any symptoms."

Buzz held up his hand for Mag to stop. He leaned in closer to the radio speaker and listened for a second. Then he turned back to Mag. "I don't know, Mag. Here's what I figure. Your family pretty much lives a sequestered life already. You hardly go to the store, because your family is so self-sufficient. Your wife home schools, and you're self employed. You had a book tour, but it was in the upper peninsula where the population density is near zero. I'm guessing you never got the first round of Covid. There's talk that this bio-weapon was designed to be triggered by Covid 19. So anyone who didn't get the first round can't get the second round."

Mag nodded his head. "Makes sense. What about you?"

The colonel laughed. "I've been anti-social for years, ever since I retired. If you weren't my neighbor I'd probably kick you out the door right now. I can't believe I'm even talking to you right now."

Mag smiled, but wondered deep down inside how

much of that was true. Buzz just didn't seem to like having company, and every time Mag was with Buzz, he always felt like he was in a hurry for him to leave.

"This new virus seems to work so fast. It's like two days and you're dead. Is that what's happening across the world?"

Buzz sipped his warm coffee. "Pretty much."

And then Mag asked him the million-dollar question. "So, when do you think it will be safe to go into the outside again?"

Buzz looked thoughtful for a moment. He reached up to run his right hand through his crew cut hair. "Well, I'm no epidemiologist, but I think it will burn itself out pretty fast. After all, it must be running out of people to infect by now. I mean look ... the Chinese may have done us a favor by nuking our big cities. Those were the hot spots, and now they're gone. No more airports, no public transit, no cabs, no schools, no restaurants, no trains, nothing. The big weakness in a virus is it's got no legs. It can't move without a host. You kill the host and the virus goes away."

Mag shifted his butt on the stool. His left cheek was starting to go numb. "Okay, well that makes sense. Sounds crude, but the reason stands up under scrutiny. The thing I'm wondering about is when we can get out and about. I'd like to get some intel on what's going on at the local level."

Buzz scratched the three-day whiskers on his chin before offering his advice. "I wouldn't be in any hurry about that if I was you. Give it a week and then re-evaluate. In the meantime catch all the chatter you can on the local Hams and CB radios." And then he paused, as if considering his words carefully. "But I wouldn't do much transmitting."

Mag crossed his arms on his chest. "Really? Why not?"

"Well, think about it. Ten percent of the world is still alive. That ten percent isn't as prepared as you and I. They're afraid, alone, hungry and desperate. Under those conditions even the best of people can do things they wouldn't normally do." The colonel sipped his tepid coffee again. "And to top it all off, there are no more restraining influences in our society. As soon as people figure out they can do anything they want with impunity ... it's Katy bar the door, cuz if you have something they want, all they have to do is overpower you and take it."

Mag nodded his head. "So we'll keep a low profile, a wait-and-see attitude. We'll gather as much electronic intel as we can before we march in where angels fear to tread."

Buzz smiled. "Well, I don't know that I've ever referred to myself as an angel, but ... yeah, that's the right idea. Let's just lay low for a while."

And then another thought occurred to Mag.

"Have you been down here nonstop since all this started?"

The colonel rubbed his bloodshot eyes before answering him. "Yeah, pretty much. I should probably shower though. I must smell awful."

"Well, I wasn't going to say anything, colonel but ..."

"Just shut up, sergeant. There's nothing worse than a non-com who says they weren't going to say anything and then have them say something stupid."

"Good point, colonel. Listen, what do you think of my son, Cypress, coming down here and listening in with you from time to time? He loves working communications, but all we have at home is the Ham radio and the CB. This way he could learn some technical stuff and I wouldn't come down here bothering you so much."

The colonel hesitated.

"Of course he'll bring a dozen fresh eggs when he comes down as well."

The colonel smiled and sipped his coffee again. "You drive a hard bargain, sergeant." And then he looked up at the cement wall as if he couldn't see it. He was quiet and Mag let him be while he was thinking. Finally, the old man nodded.

"Yeah, sure. As long as he doesn't talk too much. I don't like kids who don't know when to shut up. And if he gets good enough, maybe I'll even let him stay down here alone so I can get some sleep. I haven't slept much the past few days."

Mag got up to leave. "Is there anything else you need, colonel? You all set for supplies?"

Buzz laughed out loud. "Are you kiddin' me? I've got ammo up the butt and MREs for a lifetime." He pointed over to the corner at the pallets of MREs and another of 5.56 ammo and 9mm. The olive-drab steel ammo cases were stacked all the way to the ceiling.

Mag reached down, picked up his coffee mug and drained it before setting it back down on the comm bench with a thud.

"Thanks for the coffee, colonel."

Buzz grunted his approval and pointed toward the door. "Good. Go ahead and find your own way out. I got work to do, sergeant."

And then he turned his back on Mag and started pressing buttons and turning dials. Mag watched him for several seconds, and was amazed at his neighbor. *It's like he no longer knows I'm here.* Mag smiled and started walking up the stairs and out of the house. He closed the outer door to the house, being sure to lock it behind him, simply because he knew that was the colonel's procedure.

When he walked out onto the porch, the sun hit him full in the face. It was almost 65 degrees now with barely a whisper for a breeze. It was one of those rare and sought-after Indian summer days. Mag loved those the best. He turned and walked across the driveway and the lawn before heading back to his house. He had a lot to think about and a lot to decide. But he would talk to Karen first. She would see things that he didn't, and give him an opposing perspective.

Mag looked down the road toward town and wondered *... is there even anyone alive down there?*

Time would soon tell.

What is Short Wave?

There are very few people who own and operate short wave radios. After all, why should they? Ours is a world saturated with communication and information of every kind. We have social media, TV, cell phones and AM/FM radio. If anything, we have too much communication with the outside world. But after the apocalypse, all that will end ... eventually.

shortwave[shawrt-weyv]
noun
1. a radio wave shorter than that used in AM broadcasting, corresponding to frequencies of over 1600 kilohertz: used for long-distance reception or transmission.

dictionary.com

Shortwave radios are different than FM, cell phones, Ham and CB radios. The frequency range of shortwave generally extends from 3–30 MHz. But here's the most important thing: like an AM wave, shortwave can be bounced off the ionosphere; it's not hampered by line of sight or any obstructions. The radio wave is shot up at an angle, hits the ionosphere and bounces back down to earth. This process is called "skip" or "skywave." This is what allows shortwave radios to transmit or receive broadcasts from all over the world.

Just like any other radio, the signal strength is limited by the transmitter power and the characteristics of the antennae.

WHY IS COMMUNICATION IMPORTANT IN APOCALYPSE?

Look at it this way. You know there's danger out there, but you have no idea where it's coming from or how strong it is. Information is crucial in planning for everything in our life. After the apocalypse, intelligence gathering will be limited, but also more important than ever before. Here are some things that you'll no longer be forewarned about:

- Weather emergencies like tornadoes

- Crime in your locale

- The existence of government

Without this information you can't plan. The Jacobs family is totally cut off from the rest of the world and they are left wondering. How bad is it? How long will it last? Are we going to die? These are all important questions and can be answered with proper planning.

Shortwave receivers are fairly inexpensive and can be purchased on Amazon for under a hundred dollars or up into a few thousand dollars. Just remember that you get what you pay for.

CB, FSR, FM and Ham radios will tell you what's going on in your community, but if you want to know what's going on in the country and worldwide, then shortwave is the "wave" to go!

> *"As long as they have the disease they remain unclean. They must live alone; they must live outside the camp."*
>
> *Leviticus 13:46 (NIV)*

CHAPTER 3

The Agony of Ignorance

MAG HEARD THE CRYING AS HE approached the front porch. He recognized it as Katy, so he ran the last few paces up the steps and into the house. When he burst through the door, he saw Karen on the couch, holding their daughter in her arms.

After a quick scan for blood and finding none, he relaxed just a tad. "What's wrong with Katy?"

Karen looked up frowning. She spoke as she continued to hold her daughter, rocking her gently back and forth. "Katy still can't get ahold of her best friend, Mary. She's worried about her."

Much of what Mag was thinking couldn't be spoken aloud in front of his little daughter right now. Things like: *well, she's probably already dead like 90 percent of the rest of the planet.* But he kept his mouth shut for now. Instead, he walked over and knelt down on the carpet beside his wife and daughter, wrapped his arms around both of them and added to the group hug. Just then Michael and Cypress rushed out into the living room to see what was going on.

Katy continued to wail as Karen tried to calm her down. Mag kept thinking about what the colonel had told him about hunkering down for now. *I wouldn't be in any hurry about that if I was you. Give it a week and then re-evaluate.* He knew he should just stay home rather than go out in the community just yet, but ... and he wanted to do the right thing ... but his little caboose was in agony. All of a sudden, Mag heard his voice say, "Why don't I run over there and see what's going on?"

Karen looked up at him, alarmed. Katy's cries lessened and eventually stopped altogether. She looked up at Mag with eyes that screamed out "My Daddy is my hero!" Katy smiled and jumped off her mother's lap and into Mag's chest.

"Oh, thank you, Daddy! I miss her so much and I'm afraid she got the virus."

After a few minutes of comforting his daughter, Karen was the first to speak. "May I speak with you out on the porch, Mag?"

Mag's elation at pleasing his daughter was short-lived when he saw the death stare in his wife's eyes.

"You wait here, Caboose, while I go figure this out with Mommy, okay."

They both walked out onto the porch leaving Katy with the two boys. No sooner had Mag sat down on the porch swing when his wife started her lecture.

"Are you out of your mind!" It was less a question than a proclamation, so he didn't answer her. "You can't go out there right now! You know as well as I do that her and her whole family are probably dead from the virus, and if you go to their house you'll probably get it too!"

She continued on, detailing all the reasons he shouldn't do what he'd promised. Mag didn't interrupt her, he just let her finish. Finally, Mag was able to get a word in edge-wise, and he outlined the whole conversation he'd had with Buzz about the theories on why they hadn't died from the virus. He laid it out as compellingly as possible, despite the fact he agreed that it was best to stay home until they were sure the pathogen had burned itself out.

When Mag was finished, Karen pursed her lips togeth-er tightly and narrowed her eyes. "So, you're basically saying, Honey, I know you're right but I'm going to be stupid anyways?"

Mag smiled. Most of the time he loved her candorous way of communicating. Now was not one of those times. He nodded his head. "That's exactly what I'm saying, honey."

She fussed and fumed for several minutes more, but eventually she gave in. "Fine! Go ahead and kill yourself if you want to. Leave me a widow and the kids as orphans just so you can be hero for a day with your daughter."

She punched him in the arm several times and then broke down and cried. Mag reached over and pulled her into his chest. She resisted for a few seconds, but then let herself be drawn in to be comforted. Five minutes later they talked again and made plans together on how Mag would reconnoiter Mary's house while exposing himself to the virus as little as possible. In the end, they were both equally dissatisfied with the plan.

Bill and Susan Wright lived 2 miles from the Jacob's home, in a little ranch house up close to the main road that ran directly through Hickory Flats on the way to Plainwell and Otsego. There were just a few businesses there: the dollar store, the gas station, a little hardware and garden store and an insurance business that had been there for as long as Mag could remember.

He had to drive through town to get to the Wright's home, and the atmosphere was a bit eerie. Hickory Flats had always been a sleepy little town, quiet and crime free for the most part. Mag had grown up here as had Karen. There was a local K through 12 school, all on one campus with an enrollment of less than a thousand students. People always joked that you had to have a reason to venture to Hickory Flats, simply because there was nothing here. Most strangers who came here had ventured off the interstate in search of gas or had taken a wrong turn.

But Hickory Flats was more than sleepy now ... it was dead.

Michael was in the passenger seat of the truck beside him. "Dad, this is creepy. Where is everybody?"

Mag kept searching the streets for any sign of life, but found nothing. "I don't know, son. Just keep your eyes peeled and let me know if you see anything dangerous."

His son held tight to the AR-15 carbine standing on end with the muzzle pointing toward the ceiling of the truck cab. Mag was driving slow, about 10 miles per hour.

"What's that awful smell, Dad?"

Mag recognized it from the house on the lakeshore where he'd found the dead family just last week. "Those are dead people, son."

Michael raised the flannel cloth of his long-sleeved shirt up to his nose, but it couldn't hold out the smell.

"Look at the windows on the dollar store. They're all broken out. What does that mean?"

Mag thought about it for a second. "I guess it means we're not the only ones left alive, son. And we need to be extra careful."

Mag kept shifting his eyes from side to side and back to front. He had his own AR-15 propped up against the seat beside him and his 9mm pistol holstered on his right hip. Michael was the first to see it.

"Dad, on my side of the road up by that house."

Mag looked over and instinctively braked when he saw it. There was the body of a middle-aged man lying halfway inside the house. His head and torso were outside on the cement. Michael raised the binoculars to his eyes and cringed. "Dad! Half his face is gone!"

Michael handed the optics to his dad and leaned back hard in the cushioned seat. After looking at the body close up, Mag lowered the glasses and handed them back to his son. "Animals, son. Probably dogs. No one's feeding them anymore."

Michael swallowed hard. "You mean, like ... pets?"

Mag looked over at his son. "Not pets anymore. Dogs are part of nature, always have been. We domesticated them, but they're from the wolf family. And they're pack animals, so we need to be very careful, son."

Michael took one last look at the body and shuddered. "Okay then, important safety tip. Don't pet the nice doggie." Mag started driving again and continued past town, past the library and the fire department. It was one of those volunteer fire departments that most rural areas seemed to have. They saw two more bodies. An older woman, who was lying face down on the sidewalk, and a teen-age boy who was in the middle of the street. He had died on his back, and his face now pointed up at the September sun. Blood had pooled out all around him and had congealed days ago. Mag stepped on the brake and reached over for the binoculars. When he brought the glasses up to his eyes, he saw the stab wounds on the boy's torso. There were more than he could count. And then he recognized the boy's face. Michael reached over for the optics, but Mag told him no.

"It's Devon Collins, son."

The color drained from Michael's face. "Are you sure?"

Mag nodded. "But Dad, I was just playing basketball with him 2 weeks ago at church."

Mag looked over at his son, who couldn't seem to take his eyes off the dead body. It was one thing to see a stranger's death, or to listen to a news report about death, but ... to see someone you knew, lying in a pool of their own dried blood ... that was a different matter.

"You okay, son?"

Michael nodded blankly.

"Stay alert, son. He was stabbed to death." Mag took his foot off the brake and maneuvered around the dead body. Michael couldn't keep himself from taking a closer look at it as they passed. He almost threw up when the smell hit him, but he managed to choke it down.

At the southern outskirts of town they approached the Wright's house. Mag slowed and coasted to a stop at the end of the driveway. He couldn't believe his eyes. There on the porch, sitting in the swing was Susan Wright and Mary was beside her, rocking lightly back and forth. Michael started to jump out of the truck, but Mag held him back.

"No, son. There's something wrong with this."

Michael argued with him. "But look, Dad. That's Mary and her mom. They're alive. Let's go talk to them."

"Just wait. I promised your mom we'd be careful."

He put the truck in park and lifted the binoculars to his face. Tears filled his eyes when he realized that Susan Wright had been dead for several days. And then he moved the glasses down to young Mary. Her eyes were open, staring blankly out at the street.

"They're both dead, son."

Michael looked at him with disbelief in his eyes, so Mag handed him the binoculars. His son hesitated, not sure he wanted a closer look. He took them and looked up at the porch. There were flies buzzing all over Susan Wright's face. Then he glassed over to little Mary. All of a sudden, he brought the optics down and laid them in his lap. Then he quickly pulled them up again. He did this twice.

"What's wrong? What is it?"

Michael looked over at his dad with terror in his eyes. "Dad, her eyes are blinking."

And then, as they both watched from 50 yards away, little Mary stood up and walked back into the house.

MAG AND HIS SON SAT IN THE TRUCK FOR SEVERAL minutes wondering what to do. He'd promised not to take any chances, but ... this was Mary. Her mother had obviously died from the disease. She had the familiar sores on her face that he'd seen on the lakeshore family. Mag called Karen and spoke with her for several minutes. They agreed on a course of action, and he put down his son's cell phone.

"Stay here, son, and cover my back. Stay alert and don't let anyone sneak up on us. I'm going in to get Mary. We're taking her home with us."

Michael looked over in disbelief. "But, Dad. What if

she's infected? We could all die."

Mag shook his head. "I don't think she is. She'd have died with her mother. But just to be extra careful, when I get back, I'm going to ride in the back of the truck until we get home. I want you to roll up the cab windows, and don't get out of this truck."

He looked at Michael sternly. "Can you do that?"

His son hesitated, but finally nodded.

Mag left his carbine inside the cab and walked slowly down the sidewalk and up to the house. When he got to the porch, the smell was nearly unbearable. And then the nausea in the pit of his stomach overwhelmed him, and he turned to the left and vomited into the bushes. After wiping his mouth with his sleeve, Mag approached the front door. He purposely looked away from Susan. She and her husband had been to their house a dozen times for dinner over the past few years. They'd moved here from Chicago.

The inside steel door was open, so Mag knocked on the outer screen storm door. "Mary, it's Mag Jacobs. May I come in?"

There was silence inside the house. "Mag peeked in-side. The place was a mess. He knocked again. "Mary, it's Katy's father. May I come in?"

He waited a few more seconds, and then slowly and carefully opened the door enough to put his head inside and look around. Mary was nowhere to be seen, so he stepped inside and let the screen door close quietly behind him. He wanted to draw his pistol and clear the house room by room, but Mary was inside and he didn't want to frighten her. First, he looked in the kitchen. There were several open cans of Spaghettios on the table. They were all empty. There was a loaf of bread with some peanut butter as well. He checked the living room and then the bathroom. Mag had been here before, so he knew the layout of the house. He heard Mary's voice, so he moved down the hallway off the living room to the master bedroom. He opened the door slowly and peeked inside.

Mary was propped up with her back against the head board, sitting beside her father who had been dead for several days. The tell-tale sores were all over his face and arms. Bill's eyes were still wide open, but they were starting to dry out and sink into his eye sockets. He looked like a very realistic store mannequin.

Mary had the book open in front of her, and she read as her father listened without hearing.

"Then from the woods by the creek, a nightingale began to sing. Everything was silent, listening to the nightingale's song. The bird sang on and on. The cool wind moved over the prairie, and the song was round and clear above the grasses' whispering. The sky was like a bowl of light overturned on the flat black land."

Mag watched in tears as Mary read *Little House on the Prairie* to her dead father.

"The song ended. No one moved or spoke. Laurie and Mary were quiet, Pa and Ma sat motionless. Only the wind stirred and the grasses sighed."

Mary stopped reading and turned to her father's unmoving body. "I like that part, Daddy." And then she thought to herself before going on. "But I like it better when Mommy reads it to me."

Mag cleared his throat and Mary looked up. "Oh, hello, Mr. Jacobs. Is Katy with you?"

Mag shook his head as he spoke. "No, Mary. She's not, but she's waiting for you at our house. She asked if you'd like to come over and play dolls with her today."

Mary looked over at her dead father on the bed. She

thought about it, but then turned back to Mag.

"I would love that, but I have to stay and take care of Mommy and Daddy. They are very sick and they need me."

Mag nodded. "I understand, honey, and it's very good of you to do that for them." He paused. "But I was thinking maybe we could take them to our house for the day, that way my wife could see them and take care of them for you while you play with Katy."

Mag waited while the little girl thought about it. Finally she answered. "I would like that, but I should finish this chapter first." And then she began to read again.

"Then Pa lifted the fiddle to his shoulder and softly touched the bow to the strings. A few notes fell like clear drops of water into the stillness."

Mag listened as the little girl read. The sight was breaking his heart. He didn't like this new world, a world where friends and relatives died heinously, where teen-age boys were knifed on the streets and left to rot. But this was the world he lived in, like it or not. And, for whatever reason, not liking it wouldn't make it change.

"When the strings were silent, the nightingale went on singing. When it paused, the fiddle called to it and it sang again. The bird and the fiddle were talking to each other in the cool night under the moon."

Mary sighed and closed the book. She looked up at Mag and then over to her father. "I'll read chapter 6 later, Daddy. We're going to Katy's house now."

And then she looked up to Mag sadly. "I can't lift them. Mr. Jacobs."

Mag smiled as best he could. "That's okay, Mary. I'll carry them out to the truck. I'll be careful as I can." Mag wiped away his tears. "Go to your room now and get some books and your favorite dolls and toys. Put them in a bag so you can carry them. Your mom and dad can stay with us until they get better."

Mary said nothing. She got up and left the room. Mag wrapped Bill Wright in his blankets and picked him up as best he could. The smell was horrendous. After that, he did the same with Susan.

Mary walked out of the house with a raggedy Ann in one hand and a pillow case full of books and dolls in another. Mag came over to help her into the bed of the pick-up truck.

Michael watched in silence from inside the cab. Mary waved to him, and he waved back. Michael started the truck, put it in gear, and drove away.

Suddenly, a feeling of doom and intense sadness fell over Mag, like a pathogenic storm, and he wondered in his heart, his broken heart, *Will the nightingale ever sing again?*

THE AFTERMATH OF PLAGUE

The small village of Hickory Flats has a population of 360 people, or, should I say, "had" a population of 360 people. Now, there are only a few dozen left alive. But even 300 dead people in a small area can cause a terrible stink as well as create new problems like secondary diseases such as typhoid or smallpox. If the village of Hickory Flats is ever to be lived in again, all the bodies will have to be buried or burned. but that's not going to happen. It is the same problem to a magnified degree in cities and towns all across America. They are rotting mausoleums, places of death, disease and pathogenic nightmares. In short, they are unlivable, and, even those who survive will be forced to leave eventually to escape the disease and unsanitary conditions.

The world has never experienced a plague under these conditions before. Even the Black Death during medieval times was less horrific than Covid-19.1. There were no cities of 3 million people in the 14th century. Plus, the death rate was less than 50 percent with the Black Death, and they were able to dispose of the bodies. In our story, so many people died, there were not enough people left to even try to reclaim the cities. That will be the task of a later generation.

THE #1 RULE

prep·per /ˈprepər/
noun: prepper; plural noun: preppers

a person who believes a catastrophic disaster or emergency is likely to occur in the future and makes active preparations for it, typically by stockpiling food, ammunition, and other supplies.

Oxford Dictionary

People know that I'm a prepper, so they always ask me: "What can I do to prepare?" Of course, there are many things, too numerous to detail in a single page, so let's just talk about the number 1 thing you'll have to do to survive a total breakdown of society. I always tell people this: "Get out of the city! Get out of the city! Get out of the city!"

Of course, that means you'll need a place to go, and that's where the real problem comes in. Because most people don't have a summer home or a bug-out location, they will blindly flee to the country. They'll be bumping up against rural families who also want to survive, and all these country folk have one thing in common. They have guns and know how to use them.

To get the highest level of safety, don't live in the city; don't visit there. Just stay away. But, of course, most people can't do that. They have jobs and lives that make city life more convenient. I suggest you take a measured approach and do the best you can with what you have.

"Jesus said, "Let the little children come to me, and do not hinder them, for the kingdom of heaven belongs to such as these.""

Matthew 19:14 (NIV)

CHAPTER 4

Quarantined ... Again

F **MAG HAD TO PLAY ONE MORE**
game of Shutes and Ladders he was going to die. It
had been almost 2 days now, and he was begging to
get out of quarantine early, but his wife wouldn't budge
on the established protocol. Neither he nor Mary showed
any signs of sickness other than the cabin fever that was
driving him crazy.

Upon arriving home with little Mary, Mag had taken
her directly into his garage office where Karen and the
boys had already set up two cots with bedding. There was
water and food enough for two days and a portable camp
toilet behind a curtain in one corner of the room. It would
have been easier to set them up in separate rooms, but
neither Mag nor Karen wanted to lock Mary in a room
by herself for two days, not after all she'd been through.
From an emotional standpoint, she needed to spend time
with Katy, to play dolls, have tea parties and talk about

her parents when she was ready for it. But that would have to wait, and for right now all she had was Mag, and he was just not emotionally prepared to spend two days in a room with a 9-year-old little girl who'd just watched her parent's die from a deadly pandemic.

"Mr. Jacobs?"

"Yes, Mary." Mag already knew what she was going to ask.

"Can we come out yet?"

"Not yet, Mary."

She lost interest in the board game and started holding her raggedy Ann, rocking her back and forth. Mag hadn't seen the sun in almost two days, and he was going crazy. If he was by himself, he could have made use of the time by working on his next novel, or reading a good book.

Mag and the rest of the household had been communicating via the Family Service Radios. Mary and Katy were able to talk several times a day, and a few times they even pretended to play dolls. Mag had been amazed by the power of a small girl's imagination.

On the day of their arrival, Michael had left the two bodies in the back of the pick-up bed as instructed, then both brothers had gone to the back yard, in the right corner, by the apple tree, and had dug a single, wide grave. They had to dig it at least 6 feet deep, and it had taken them several hours. They hadn't finished until after dark. Then, while the others were safe inside the house for the night, Mag had taken to the grizzly task of dragging the Collin's bodies out to the grave and dumping them in. They had been friends, and it seemed irreverent to just throw them into the hole, but ... that was all he could do on his own. They were too heavy for him to lower them down gently. In the end, Mag had worked long into the night piling dirt on top of Mary's mom and dad. When he was done, there was a mound of dirt that would settle after several fall rains. They would put a cross on top, but not tonight. Mag had stood beside the grave, alone in the dark, wondering, *how much worse is this going to get?* And then another thought had occurred to him. *We're alive!* And then he'd suddenly felt ashamed of his self-pity. He'd survived the pandemic, being lost and adrift on Lake Michigan, a firefight against overwhelming odds, and now, the pandemic again. So he'd returned silently to the quarantine room where Mary was sleeping.

While Mag watched Mary rock her little doll, all feelings of self and pity left him and were transferred to the little girl before him. She'd lost her parents, her home, her way of life. And then he was reminded of listening to the Michael W Smith song while floating in the middle of Lake Michigan. Nothing had changed since then. Nothing important, anyway. He still had a purpose, and Mary, lost and alone, orphaned by a deadly pathogen had now become a part of his purpose to live and smile and thrive.

"Would you like to hear a song, Mary?"

The little girl didn't look up. She just nodded. "Okay. If it's a good one."

Mag leaned over and looked through his CD collection until finding the right one. He popped it into the DVD rom drive on his laptop, and Media Player automatically came up. He advanced until coming to the right track, turned up the volume and listened.

The wind is moving
But I am standing still
A life of pages
Waiting to be filled

A heart that's hopeful
A head that's full of dreams
But this becoming
Is harder than it seems

Mary stopped rocking her doll and looked over at the laptop. She moved closer to the speaker and listened intently as the song played. Neither Mag nor Mary said a word; they just listened. Mag closed his eyes. Mary saw this and copied him. Suddenly, Mag felt the little girl crawl up onto his lap and snuggle into his chest as close as she could get. Mag hesitated. He suddenly felt clumsy, like a wooden soldier with arms that wouldn't bend. But he struggled through it and forced himself to move forward.

Mag put his arms around the little girl and gave her comfort. And, at that moment, he vowed to protect her, to love her, and to accept her into his family. She was a Jacobs now.

As the song played, Mag was reminded of a scripture verse.

"The Lord is close to the brokenhearted and
saves those who are crushed in spirit."

Psalm 34:18 (NIV)

This tiny waif of a child had been broken and crushed, but Mag and his family would nurture her, would love her and nurse her back to health so she could find her place in this brave new world.

And then the chorus came up and Mag started to sing along.

Looking for a reason
Roaming through the night to find
My place in this world

My place in this world

And then, to his surprise, Mary started to sing with him. And her voice was beautiful and full of youth and hope. Mag was reminded of another verse in the Bible.

"Start children off on the way they should go, and even when they are old they will not turn from it."

Proverbs 22:6 (NIV)

And from that day forth, Mag committed himself to teaching little Mary the way she should go, and her place in this world. She would be loved, honored and cherished.

And then Mag suddenly realized, *She is teaching me more than I can ever return.* He continued to hug her gently and rock back and forth with the song. And, when it was over, she asked him to play it again ... and again ... and again.

Saying Good Bye

THE FUNERAL SERVICE FOR BILL AND SUSAN COLLINS was small, unassuming, and beautiful. It was on the second morning after the quarantine had ended, and the sun came out with another rare day of seventy degrees and sunny. Mary stood before the grave, holding Katy's hand as she looked down at the mound of dirt. Her and Katy had picked flowers for an hour and laid them atop the dirt in little piles. There were pink flowers, red, blue and purple. Some of the white ones weren't flowers at all but just weeds that looked pretty to them.

Mary cried softly again. It lasted for several minutes. All the psychiatrists and therapists were dead, so Katy held her friend tight and grieved with her. In this new world, there would be no more counselors, emotional support animals or emotional "safe" zones. This new world would be survived by the tough and by those with friends and family and a faith in God and each other.

Mary looked over at Katy. Katy handed her the copy of *Little House on the Prairie*. She opened the book to the book marker and read aloud as Colonel Buzz and the Jacob's family listened.

> *"It was nearly noon then. The sun was almost overhead. So Laura and Mary picked flowers from the weeds, and they took the flowers to Ma, instead of a gopher.*
>
> *Ma was folding the dry clothes. The little panties and petticoats were whiter than snow, warm from the sun, and smelling like the grass. Ma laid them in the wagon, and took the flowers. She admired equally the flowers that Laura gave her, and the flowers that Mary gave her, and she put them together in a tin cup full of water. She set them on the wagon-step to make the camp look pretty."*

Mary stopped reading and closed the book. "Mommy, I'll come to you everyday with new flowers. And Daddy, I'll read to you. Just like you read to me."

Then she backed away and bowed her head. The Jacobs family as well as the colonel followed her lead. This was all her doing, her script that she'd written herself. You see, Mary was a very capable 9-year-old little girl. She raised her head and nodded to Katy before lowering it again. And Katy began to pray.

"Hello, God. Thank you for saving Mary's life. We

wish you would've saved her mommy and daddy too, but ... you must've needed them for something else." She paused as if deciding what else to say. "But I want to thank you for my new sister. She is special to me. We are going to play dolls now and have some tea. But we will always be back to read to them, so please make sure they can hear us. That's all we got today. Amen."

The adults raised their heads and looked at each other. Mag smiled. Karen smiled. The colonel smiled inside. And then Katy and Mary ran off to play.

And that was the end of the funeral.

FUNERALS DURING APOCALYPSE

In modern times funerals are a big business. In fact, dying is very expensive these days. We are forbidden by health and sanitation laws to bury our own loved ones. We must either pay a few thousand dollars to have them cremated, or five to six figures for a conventional funeral and burial.

We have to pay for a tiny plot of land to bury the body. We have to pay the funeral home for embalming, caskets, the service, and a host of other options should you choose. About the only thing more expensive than dying is getting married.

But it wasn't always like this. Prior to the American Civil War, there was no such thing as embalming. The body was prepared by the family. They were dressed up and cleaned, and the body was displayed in a room called the parlor. The parlor was a room off to the side of most houses that was rarely used except for special occasions like entertaining guests and for funerals. Of course, the life expectancy in the first half of the 19th century was much shorter than it is today, so funerals were a normal part of life. Instead of a fancy casket costing tens of thousands of dollars, a wooden casket was usually purchased from the local general store. Sometimes, if money was short, and time allowed, the casket would be home made.

However, during the apocalypse, especially death by disease, the Jacobs family is forced to go back in time almost 200 years in the way they handle the dead. First off, there should be no physical contact with the body for fear of spreading the disease. That's why Mag was the only one to move the bodies. Second, the bodies had to be buried immediately for the same health reasons. Bodies in 70-degree heat begin to decompose after just a few hours and smell quite badly. Also, rotting bodies can be host to all manner of viral and bacterial infections.

I sometimes joke with my wife that she should just bury me out back, but, if I had my druthers, and the government aside, that's exactly what I'd prefer. I wish we could go back to family cemeteries. Instead, we've turned it into a big business, and have a desire to tuck our dead away so as not to remind us of our final destination. But the bottom line is this: we are all mortal and all of us will die.

Now that the apocalypse has arrived, the 10 percent who are left living will be doing things the old-fashioned way. Funerals will be quick, small and much more personal.

> *"You shall not steal."*
>
> *Exodus 20:15 (NIV)*

CHAPTER 5

Making a Plan

THAT VERY NIGHT **M**AG CALLED A family meeting. Karen made popcorn, and the entire family sat around the dying television. Despite the fact that it was never turned on anymore, it was still the focus of the living room, the center of their attention, like an idol of old that was losing its icy grip on their lives. And Mag had been wondering about that lately. Perhaps having no television wasn't such a bad thing after all.

Cypress was on the carpeted floor with his back leaned up against the couch. Katy and Mary were seated in the recliner beside each other, holding their respective favorite dolls. Michael was beside his Uncle Johnny on the couch. Everyone shared popcorn from a large stainless steel bowl that was being passed from one person to another. Karen was seated in the wooden rocking chair, with Mag between her ankles on the floor with his back up against the face of the chair. Mag started the meeting with prayer.

"Dear, Lord God, we thank you for life. We used to take that for granted, but not anymore. Thanks for all you've given us. Please guide us as we plan for the future. Amen."

And then he looked around the room and smiled. "I'm glad that we're all together again. When I was out there floating on Lake Michigan, I almost lost hope that I'd make it back here to my family." He looked down at his hands. "But I did, and I thank God for that." He looked up again at everyone eating popcorn. It was like he was the center of the movie. "There are some things we need to talk about." He hesitated. "First, we need to plan for the future. Second, we need to talk about security, and last but not least, we need to talk about our feelings."

His brother, Johnny, looked up from the popcorn bowl and shrugged. "Talk about our feelings? In public? Why would we do that?"

Karen reached her hand down and ran her fingers through Mag's hair. "I told you he'd say that." And then she laughed.

Michael started to say something, but Mag held his hand up to silence him. "It's not mandatory, but if you want to talk about things that are bothering you inside, then we can do that." And then he smiled mischievously at his brother. "We already know that your Uncle Johnny has no feelings, so we'll just skip him."

Karen playfully slapped the top of her husband's head. "Don't say that, Mag." And then she paused before adding. "Even if it is true."

"Let's start with the planning part then. We'll just go around the room and we all can have our say on what we think needs to be done around here."

He pointed at Michael. "We'll start with you, son."

Michael paused. "I don't like going first."

"That's okay, but someone has to go first and you're the oldest. What do you think we should change around here?"

His oldest son thought for a moment while everyone else passed around the popcorn bowl. "Well, I think we need to figure out who's dead and who's alive around here. Maybe not all the way into town, but at least our closest neighbors. For example, Mr. and Mrs. Clyborg two houses down. They don't have any family close by and they're old. Someone should go check on them."

Mag nodded. He picked up the pen and paper tablet that was on the coffee stand beside the rocker and wrote it down. Then he laid the tablet down on his lap.

"Good suggestion, Michael." Then he nodded at Cypress. "You're next, son."

Cypress turned slightly sideways on the floor so that his right side was pressed up against the couch. "I want to know what's going on out there too. You mentioned I might be able to help the colonel with comms, but it hasn't happened yet. I think we need to get that done."

Michael reached down and flicked his brother's right ear playfully. "You just want to eat up the man's MREs. that's all."

Irritated, Cypress pushed his brother's hand away. "No way, man. I just want to help."

Mag silenced them both, then he wrote it down. "Okay, good suggestion." He pointed at his brother, Johnny. Johnny looked at him and smiled, wondering whether or not to crack a joke.

"Well, there's a dire lack of snack cakes and beer

around here that I find rather alarming."

The two boys laughed out loud, but their mother silenced them with her patented death stare. Johnny quickly backtracked. Mag wanted to smile, but he knew better. He just waited for his brother to get serious.

"Well, I was thinking about electricity."

Mag cocked his head quizzically to one side. "What do you mean? What's wrong with the electricity?"

Johnny looked over at his brother in disbelief. "Do you mean to tell me that you actually believe the electricity is going to keep pumping into this house indefinitely? I can't believe it hasn't shut off already."

Mag thought about it and looked up and over his shoulder at Karen. "Guess I hadn't gotten around to thinking about that part yet. To be honest with you, I always knew it would happen, but there's so much else we have to do that I'm just taking it day by day. But you're right, we need to plan for it." And then he looked over at the two boys. "Is the internet still up?"

Michael was the first to speak. "Well, it's spotty. Some pages you look for are coming up with error messages. Others come up just fine. But some don't come up at all."

And then Cypress chimed in. "And social media is toast. You can forget about FaceBook."

Young Katy looked up from her doll. "What's FaceBook?"

Mag smiled. "Nothing of any consequence, Caboose. At least not anymore." And then he added. "May social media rest in peace."

"So what are we going to do about the electricity? The power could go off any second now."

Mag answered his brother as he thought. "Well, I have a generator, but it runs on gas. I'd prefer to save that for the chainsaws and the truck."

Johnny added. "Gas starts to go bad after about 8 months. Unless you put stabilizer in it."

Mag nodded. "That's true. This is going to be a problem. This changes everything." He glanced over at Johnny. "How long do you think we have before the power goes out?"

Johnny shrugged. "Like I said, it could go out at any moment. The problem is no one's minding the store."

Michael chimed in. "What does that mean?"

"It means all the people who used to keep the power plants running are either dead or just not showing up for work. Creating energy takes fuel, so when there's no one to load in the fuel, then the generators stop making electricity." He paused. "I'd say we're living on borrowed time when it comes to electricity."

And then Mag looked up at his wife again. "Honey, how are we set for food? Do we have enough to get us through the winter?"

She nodded. "Yeah, I think so. But I'd feel better if we had more." And then she looked over at her brother-in-law. "And if we lose power like Johnny thinks we will, then what happens to all our meat? We've got two chest freezers. One is almost empty because the venison is almost gone, but the other is packed with beef, pork, turkey and chicken." She looked back down at Mag. "As soon as the electricity goes out, we got about 48 hours before it all starts to rot."

And that was the moment everyone finally realized how tough it was going to be in the apocalypse. None of them had ever lived without electricity before; at least not for more than a few days.

For the next 2 hours they made a plan. And then they

began to carry it out.

"HONEY, I THINK IT'S SAFE TO ASSUME THAT I'M not going to get Covid 19.1, simply because I've been exposed so much and haven't got it yet. We know the incubation period is just a few hours, and that the infected person dies in two days." He pointed at his chest with both hands. "Honey, I'm not dead yet. I'm not even sick."

Karen sighed in defeat. She didn't want him to leave the house and go into town, but she couldn't argue with his logic. It was sound. They needed more jars and lids if they were going to can all that meat. Finally, she gave in.

"Okay, but you promise me that Johnny stays in the truck and has no contact with anyone."

Mag nodded. "Of course. And, if for any unforeseen reason he makes contact, then he goes into quarantine for two days."

And then Karen's frown turned into a smile. "Well, now that wouldn't be so bad, would it? Two days without your brother's stupid jokes and bad sense of humor."

Mag laughed. "I should have known you'd find a silver lining to all this."

And then her face grew stern again. "Just one more stipulation. "He doesn't bring home any beer."

Mag reached over and held her tight. "I got it, babe. Not a problem."

He said good bye to the kids, made sure the day's security watch was set, and then he and his brother hopped into the truck and drove to town. They were both decked out in full battle gear. Tactical vests with body armor as well as their sidearms and AR-15 carbines.

On the way into town, Johnny asked his brother a question. "How are we going to buy canning jars and lids if the people who own the store are dead?"

Mag thought about that for a second, and he was reminded of two weeks earlier when he'd needed a rubber raft to float across the Mackinaw straits. In retrospect, he may have made a mistake there. He could have died because of his adherence to the law. But that had been a different time. It was amazing how much could change in the course of just a few days during the apocalypse.

Back then there had still been a thread of law and order, but ... now ... he hadn't seen a cop since he'd left St. Ignace.

"Well, here's what I decided when I was trying to make my way home from the upper peninsula. It's simple, but it seems to work. Here it is: no one innocent gets hurt, and no one gets cheated."

Johnny thought about it for a few seconds. "Okay, that's a nice little rule, but what exactly does that look like in real life?"

"Mag slowed as they approached town. "It means if the store owner is alive, then we make him an honest deal. If he's dead, then we assume the merchandise is no longer owned. Therefore, it's not stealing and no one gets hurt by it."

Johnny nodded. "Makes sense. You could even argue that if we don't take it, then our family could die from hunger."

Mag nodded. "I know it's a bit dicey, but that's all I got, bro."

The blue, water tower was in view now. "Better stay alert. We don't know what we're driving into."

Johnny pulled the short carbine up onto his lap and stuck the muzzle up at a 45-degree angle outside the window. Mag's eyes darted fervently back and forth as they pulled up to a stop in front of the hardware store.

"I'll go inside. Remember, you stay out here and watch my back. If you see anything dangerous, just yell and I'll come on out."

His brother opened the sun roof on the cab and stuck his head out the top as he assumed the overwatch position.

Mag approached the front door to the hardware store slowly. He'd been here hundreds of times in his life, but never like this, not holding a carbine and suited up for a possible war. The glass windows in front were broken and so was the glass front door. The busted glass chips crunched under the weight of his black, combat boots. When he reached the door, he placed his body in line with the door frame for cover. Then he yelled inside.

"Hey Brody! You in there?" There was no answer. He couldn't tell by smell whether or not a dead body was inside, because the entire town reeked of rotting corpses.

"Brody, it's Mag Jacobs. You in there?"

Still no answer. Mag looked back at his brother to make sure he was alert. "Brody, I'm coming in now. Don't shoot me, okay."

He walked slowly inside the shadows of the store, and soon Johnny lost him from view. Inside, the smell got stronger. Mag moved as quietly as possible, moving from cover to cover as best he could. That's when he saw the dark figure beside Brody's body. Mag covered his nose with his left sleeve. The body was bloated and was being chewed and torn by a large, black dog, some kind of pitpull-shepherd mix. The dog's shoulders were huge as it latched on with its jaws and shook its head from side to side, tearing out chunks of meat.

Mag hadn't expected this. It was odd; he'd been prepared to kill a man, but he wasn't quite ready to shoot a dog yet. He yelled as loud as he could.

"Go on! Get out of here!"

The dog looked up and growled, baring his bloody teeth. An unexpected coldness suddenly ran though Mag's veins. He raised his carbine up and pointed it at the dog just to be safe. "Go on now! Get out of here or I'm gonna have to shoot you!"

The dog took a step closer. "Go on! Git!"

It was at that moment when Mag realized that the dog was no longer afraid of him. To the contrary, he saw Mag not as the ruling class, not as a pet owner, but as a piece of meat. The dog lunged straight toward him.

Instinctively, Mag pressed the trigger three times. The first two shots hit him in the chest, but didn't stop the dog's attack. The final bullet struck the big dog in the head, and he collapsed immediately.

Mag stood over the dog's body, his hands shaking. He pushed the dog's head with his boot just to check. Then he realized that his brother was yelling at the front of the store. "Mag! You okay! I'm coming in!"

Mag didn't answer him. For some reason he was having trouble talking. A few seconds later, Johnny was standing beside him with his AR-15 raised.

"Holy schnipes that's a big dog."

And then he saw the dead body by the counter. He looked over at his brother. "Is that Brody Connors?"

Mag nodded. "What's left of him."

Johnny shook his head from side to side. "You didn't shoot him, did you?"

Mag appeared perturbed. He was already pretty upset about killing the dog. "Of course not. The dog was eating him and then he attacked me."

Johnny looked him up and down. "You okay?"

Mag nodded. "Let's just get what we came for and get out of here."

It took them 15 minutes to find the jars and load them into the truck.

"Listen, Mag. He didn't sell guns, but I know he had some ammo and some hunting stuff here. We should check it out."

Mag agreed and they went into the back storage room. Mag had never been here before, and he felt like he was intruding, despite the fact that the owner was already dead. There was a desk with papers on top of it. He opened all the drawers and looked for anything they might need. He found a box of 38 special rounds in the pencil drawer and took them.

Out in the display room, Johnny took some rakes and hoes as well as gas cans, trash bags and assorted nuts and bolts and hand tools. As they were leaving, Mag saw the two-man bull saw standing up in the corner.

"Wait, Johnny. Get that bull saw. Our chainsaws won't work forever. We'll need that for cutting wood."

While Johnny got the saw, plus two others, Mag walked over and looked down at Brody's body. He took a broom handle and rolled him over onto his back.

"What are you doing, bro? He's dead. Show some respect."

Mag covered his mouth with one hand and reached down with the other. He pulled the 38 special revolver out of the dead man's inside the waistband holster, wiped the blood and ooze off of it the best he could, and shoved it into his pocket.

"Johnny, let's go to the dollar store and see what they have there."

Johnny saw the wild look in his brother's eyes and decided not to argue with him. They loaded everything into the truck and drove across the street and parked in the lot. The scene was similar. Broken glass, a few dead bodies. These people were from out of town, so Mag didn't recognize them. The smell was even worse in this store. This time, they both walked in with carbines raised.

Karen had wanted cleaning supplies, so they grabbed two shopping carts and loaded them both up with laundry detergent, toilet paper, wipes, ammonia, bleach, bar soap, dental floss, tooth brushes, tooth paste and a lot of rubbing alcohol. Then Mag topped off the cart with cold medicines, pain relievers, bandages, antibacterial ointment and last, but not least, feminine napkins for his wife.

Johnny looked down at the last item and smiled. Mag frowned. "Not a word, bro. Especially while I'm holding a gun."

Johnny shrugged and walked up to the check-out lane. "I'm just gonna pay for this and move on. Plenty of time to tease you later on."

Mag followed him with his own cart. That's when they heard the crunch of glass behind them. An instant later there was a loud BOOM, and the rack of paperback books fell over beside Mag, with pieces of paper flying all over him. Mag fell to the floor.

"Don't move, either of you, or I'll kill ya both!"

The Law of the Jungle

law of the jungle
noun
a system or mode of action in which the strongest survive, presumably as animals in nature or as human beings whose activity is not regulated by the laws or ethics of civilization.

dictionary.com

Now that most people are dead, and the landscape is littered with supplies for the taking, Mag and his family have to be very careful about how they proceed, lest they descend into lawlessness. The Bible says "Thou shall not steal." But is it stealing in this scenario? While Mag was in the upper peninsula, prior to societal collapse, law and order was still in force, so he left money before taking the rubber raft. But now ... the owners are dead, and that changes everything.

Mag's new law states: "no one innocent gets hurt, and no one gets cheated."

This new guideline is to become vitally important in the weeks to come. Compromising on morality can become a very slippery slope, so the Jacob's family must adhere to this new rule or they could become the evil that they hate.

THE LAW FOR THE WOLVES

EXCERPT FROM POEM

"NOW this is the law of the jungle, as old and as true as the sky,

And the wolf that shall keep it may prosper, but the wolf that shall break it must die.

As the creeper that girdles the tree trunk, the law runneth forward and back;

For the strength of the pack is the wolf, and the strength of the wolf is the pack."

—Rudyard Kipling (1865–1936)

> *"Of them the proverbs are true: "A dog returns to its vomit,"and, "A sow that is washed returns to her wallowing in the mud.""*
>
> *2 Peter 2:22 (NIV)*

CHAPTER 6

Dollar Store Disaster

MAG LAY FACE DOWN ON THE floor of the dollar store, bits of paper still floating down around him. He rolled onto his back and hoisted up his AR-15 to his chest. Then he heard Johnny rise up on the broken glass to his right and begin to fire off round after round in quick succession.

Mag rolled to his left and dashed to the cover of the aisle number three. Then he raised to one knee and brought up his carbine, firing toward the direction of the shotgun blast. He'd already fired off 10 rounds before he heard the man screaming.

"Stop shootin'! I give up, man! I give up! Just stop shootin' at me."

It was then that Mag recognized the man's voice. He yelled over to his brother. "Johnny, stop shooting. I think I know this guy."

Mag stayed behind cover. "Jerry? Is that you? It's Mag

Jacobs."

The man's voice was frantic, and he was almost in tears. "I didn't know it was you, man. I gotta protect my beer."

Mag thought for a moment. Jerry was the Hickory Flats town drunk. Every small town had at least one. He lived here in town in a small ranch house off main street with his aging mother.

"I need you to put the shotgun down, Jerry, and come on out where we can see you. Keep your hands out in the open."

They heard the shuffle of feet and broken glass. First they saw the man's hands raise up over the end cap, then he stood up slowly. "Don't shoot me, Mag."

"Jerry, are you alone?"

The man nodded. "Yeah, Mom died three days ago."

Mag shook his head. He'd gone to school with Jerry, and he'd kind of drifted after high school, never really finding his niche in the world. For the past 15 years he'd taken to the bottle and assorted drugs and been in and out of trouble with the law.

Mag stood up and Johnny followed suit. Johnny spoke next. "For cryin' out loud, Jerry. You mean to tell me that you'd get in a gun fight over a case of beer?"

Jerry was in his early forties, but a hard life had aged him beyond his years. He looked frail and skinny, like an old man before his time.

"Of course I would. I"m an alcoholic and this here's the last beer in town. I done already drank everything else."

Johnny glanced over at his brother and smiled. They both lowered their carbines. Mag walked toward him.

"You shouldn't drink so much, Jerry. It's not good for

you. And I'm sorry about yer mom." He quickly glanced outside to make sure no one else was coming up to the store after the gun fire. "We weren't taking any beer. We just came for cleaning supplies and personal hygiene stuff."

Jerry looked at their carts. "Well how was I supposed to know that? I just figured you was takin' my beer, so I had to stop ya."

For a moment, Mag thought about it, and it made sense that a lifelong alcoholic would be willing to kill for a drink of alcohol. He sighed and looked over at Jerry with a sense of pity.

"You can have all the beer. We don't want any."

Jerry took a step forward and looked again at the shopping carts. He frowned when he saw the feminine hygiene products in Mag's cart.

"Why you takin' all the Kotex?"

Johnny burst out laughing. "Yeah, that's what I was asking him too. Boy, I tell ya. Just when you think you know someone, they go and do something weird like that."

Jerry smiled for the first time and showed his jagged, brown and rotting teeth. "Yeah. That's some weird stuff, man." Mag shrugged it off, ignoring them both.

"How many people have you seen left alive here in Hickory Flats?"

Jerry turned back to him and ran his gnarled, wrinkled hand through his long, greasy, salt-and-pepper grey hair. "I ain't seen nobody local ceptin' you two. There was a whole gang a strangers come in three days ago and shot up the place. Most people were dead already er sick, so no body put up much of a fight. They killed most everbody that was still healthy. I hid in the trees till they was gone."

Mag looked over at Johnny with concern in his eyes. His brother frowned. "You haven't seen them since?"

"Nope. I don't think they'll come back. They got what they wanted 'n moved on to the next town. They was addicts I think."

That's when Johnny stepped forward. He let the carbine drop and hang on the sling in front of him. "So where's all the Twinkies and the snack cakes, Jerry. I don't see any in here."

Jerry lowered his head in shame. "Sorry, Johnny. I done ate 'em all."

Johnny looked over at his brother in disbelief, then back at Jerry. "You ate every last snack cake in town?"

He nodded. "Yep. I cleaned out here and the gas station too. I need the sugar. Gives me energy. The beer gives me carbs."

Johnny shook his head from side to side in disgust. Then he turned and walked back out to the truck, pushing his shopping cart in front of him.

Jerry looked over at Mag. "What's wrong with yer brother?"

Mag smiled sympathetically. "He'll be okay. It's a personal problem. He's just grieving a loss right now."

Jerry nodded. "Yeah. I get that. Me too."

Mag walked over and slapped Jerry on the right shoulder. "Anything you need, Jerry?"

Jerry looked off to the front of the store and relaxed his face into a frown. "Nah. I was just sleepin' in back when I heard ya all up here. I didn't know it was you, I swear."

Mag said his good byes and wheeled his shopping cart out of the store to the truck. They loaded up the supplies and Mag threw both shopping carts in back for good measure. "We may need those later."

He turned to Johnny. "Listen, bro. We need to head on out to Brody's house. It's just about a mile outside of town to the east. His wife and mom might still be alive. If they are, then we can pay them for the stuff we took from the hardware store."

Johnny nodded his head. "Yeah, seems fair."

They drove out of town and saw no one else. They pulled into Brody's drive and parked.

"Let me knock on the door first. They're more likely to recognize me than you."

Johnny remained inside the cab of the truck while Mag stepped out and walked to the door. He left his carbine in the truck and concealed his pistol under his shirt. Mag knocked loudly on the door.

"Mrs. Connors? It's Mag Jacobs. Are you home?"

He listened intently, but there was no sound from inside. He knocked again. "It's Mag Jacobs. We just came from the store. Is anyone home?" Still no answer. He walked around the house to the left and peeked through the window into the living room. He could see no one inside.

He heard Johnny slam the cab door and walk up to the front of the house. "Did you try the door knob?" Johnny reached out and twisted the door handle, and it opened easily. He looked over at Mag and nodded before slowly and carefully stepping inside. "Mrs. Connors, it's Johnny Jacobs. Don't shoot or anything. We just came to make sure you're okay."

Mag drew his pistol and walked in behind his brother. Johnny moved left while Mag stepped to the right as they cleared the living room. "Clear left." Mag responded. "Clear right."

Johnny led as they walked first to the kitchen, then the

bathroom. Nothing was out of place, and the house was immaculate. The smell of death was faint.

"Maybe no one's here. I don't smell any strong odors."

Johnny nodded in agreement. "Let's just clear the whole house and then we can get out of here."

Fifteen minutes later they'd cleared the upstairs as well as the basement. "It's like they haven't been here in days."

Mag nodded. "Maybe they were out of town when all this went down."

"Yeah. One way to find out. I'll check for cars." Johnny moved to his right, down the hallway to the garage door entrance. He opened it slowly and peeked out into the dimness. The only light coming in was through the back window. He reached around where the light switch would normally be and flicked it on.

"Mag! You'd better come see this!"

Mag rushed down the hall way and looked into the garage. He could still smell the faint odor of carbon monoxide. Inside the car sat Mrs. Connors and her mother-in-law. They were wearing their Sunday best, and the younger Mrs. Connors was slumped over the steering wheel. Brody's mother was in the front, passenger seat with a Bible open on her lap. Her face was a funny, blue color. Mag walked over and looked in through the open window. There was a verse underlined, and Mag read it to himself.

"You, however, will go to your ancestors in peace and be buried at a good old age."

Genesis 15:15 (NIV)

"Hey, Mag! Look up here." Johnny reached over to the windshield on the driver's side and took the sheet of notebook paper from underneath the wiper blade.

"Listen to this."

> To whom it may concern.
> Brody is dead and this world is ending.
> There is nothing left for us here.
> We would rather die peacefully than
> at the hands of violent, evil men.
> We can hear the gunfire getting closer now.
> Whoever finds this. Please honor our last request.
> We'd like to be buried in the back yard.
> Use the tractor in the pole barn to save your back.
> And, if you'd be so kind, please find Brody and
> bring him home to us as well. Please put a marker
> on the grave, and give us a Christian service.
> I know that's a lot to ask, but, in return,
> you may have any of our worldly possessions that
> you like. We won't be needing them.
>
> Best regards.
>
> Emma and Edna Connors.

The letter was written in an elegant hand, and Johnny was impressed with the fine penmanship. Mag wondered why the dead bodies didn't reek as bad as the others they'd found. He wondered if, perhaps, the carbon monoxide hadn't preserved them somehow. It didn't matter.

Mag looked over at his brother. "Well, at least we know how to pay our debt. "I'm gonna go fire up that tractor and start digging."

Johnny nodded. "Good idea. I'll go inside and look for anything else that might be useful."

On the way out to the pole barn, Mag called Cypress on the CB radio to give a situation report. The call went quickly as they never bothered to use call signs any more.

It took Mag only about 30 minutes to get the tractor running and dig the hole. It was a mid-sized Kubota with a front-end loader and a small back hoe. He found himself feeling guilty about making plans for all the Connor's belongings. Mag had always dreamed of buying a piece of equipment like this, but knew he'd never be able to afford it. Now he was getting one for just a few hours work. He didn't like profiting over the death of his friends and neighbors. But he forced himself to do it for the sake of his own family.

While Mag was digging the hole, his brother took load after load of items from the house and into the pick-up bed. He even had to load some into the extended cab. Brody had been an avid hunter his whole life, so they were the new owners of about 30 guns and a huge assortment of ammunition. Mag was pleased to see two sets of night vision goggles as well as two night vision scopes that Brody must've used for coyote hunting.

When it was all loaded into the truck, the two brothers stood out on the cement driveway. "How you wanna do this, big brother?"

Mag sighed and steeled himself for the task to come. "Go inside and open the garage door. I'll get the front-end loader and we'll use it to carry them to the grave."

Johnny did his part then carefully wrapped the two women in two, large blue poly tarps. Mag scooped them up and lowered them into the hole as carefully as he could. "Let's go get Brody now."

It took them almost an hour to drive the tractor to the store, then load up the owner into the front bucket. Mag and Johnny dragged out the body with ropes so they wouldn't have to touch the smelly, sticky mess. Mag waited while his brother threw up inside, making the smell even worse. On the way back to the Connor's house, the two brothers said nothing. They just wanted to get through the ordeal and return to the family.

Mag deposited the last body into the hole, shut down the tractor, and then both men stood over the grave. It was a beautiful, sunny day, almost 70 degrees again. Mag read from the Bible they'd found in the car. First, he read the passage from Genesis 15:5 that Edna had underlined in her Bible, and then another of his own choosing.

> *"By the sweat of your brow you will eat your food until you return to the ground, since from it you were taken; for dust you are and to dust you will return."*

> *Genesis 3:19 (NIV)*

And then the men bowed and prayed.

"Dear Lord, we commend this fine, Christian family into your hands. I know you have a divine plan, but I have no idea why you take some and leave others. These were good people in life. But they're with you now. We trust in you, even when we don't understand." And then Mag added. "Especially when we don't understand."

Johnny said amen, and then hopped up onto the tractor. He followed Mag home. It was slow going, but only a few miles. As soon as they got there, Johnny went into the pole barn bedroom to serve his two days quarantine.

Mag went inside, took a hot shower and changed into clean clothes. Then he stayed in his bedroom, avoiding his family for several hours.

THE INTERNAL COMBUSTION ENGINE?

internal-combustion engine
   noun
an engine of one or more working cylinders in which the process of combustion takes place within the cylinders.

dictionary.com

There are just a handful of inventions that have revolutionized humanity, and the Internal Combustion Engine ICE) is one of them. Without it, there would be no manned flight, no space flight, no cars, trucks, no practical way of harnessing electricity for our homes and for other industrial purposes.

Mag and his family is faced with the prospect of life without electricity ... possibly for the rest of their lives. Think about it. The Internal Combustion Engine is the foundation for so many other technological advances. Certainly computers were a huge milestone in advancing man's knowledge and civilization, but without the ICE to drive it, without that baseline to manufacture all the advances of the 19th and 20th centuries, things like computers, airplanes, cell phones, and cars would never have been practical for the common man. One could argue that science discovers the technology of God, but it's the engineer who transforms that technology and knowledge into something useful by the masses.

HOW TO MAKE FUEL LAST

In Mag's new world there is a glut of gasoline and diesel fuel as well as millions of internal combustion engines that are powered by these fuels. All Mag has to do is collect it. Or, he could just let it store inside underground fuel tanks at gas stations and even in cars. After all, there are millions of them across the country. But here's the big problem: most gasoline is a mixture of gas and ethanol. E10 gas is 10 percent ethanol, E15 is 15 percent and E85 is 85 percent ethanol. These fuels will last only 1 to 3 months even when properly stored because the ethanol will oxidize quickly. Ethanol is also hydrophilic, which means it will absorb moisture, and gas and water do not mix.

REC90 gas has no ethanol and will last over a year if properly stored. This is commonly referred to as recreational fuel and is used in motor boats.

Diesel fuel can last one to three years when properly stored. The enemies to all types of fuel are as follows:

- Higher temperatures

- Water (from condensation in the tanks)

- Bacterial/fungal growth

The key to fuel longevity is to store the fuel at temperatures below 70 degrees in an underground tank. You can also add a fuel stabilizer. The most well-known is called Sta-bil and can be purchased on Amazon. (But not after the apocalypse.)

"As the sun was setting, Abram fell into a deep sleep, and a thick and dreadful darkness came over him.

Genesis 15:12 (NIV)

CHAPTER 7

<u>*The Night the Lights went out*</u>

THERE ARE SEMINAL MOMENTS IN every person's life. For many, it is their marriage to another person; or, the birth of their first child. When these moments occur, their lives are changed irrevocably forever. In some regards, it is a miniature TEOTWAWKI situation, that is, 'The End of the World as We Know it.'

Intellectually, the Jacobs family thought they were ready for a world without electricity, but they were mistaken.

It was 9pm and they were sitting in the living room, having a family meeting. They'd spent the last two days canning meat from the freezer in anticipation of this very event. But the freezer was still half full. Katy and Mary were the first to react. Katy screamed, but Mary simply cowered down into the seat cushion. Katy ran to Karen and jumped on her lap. "Mommy! Is this the darkness? Is the electricity gone?"

Karen stroked her head, trying to calm her. Michael slid over beside little Mary and put his arm around her. "It's okay, little one. Nothing to be afraid of."

Cypress got up from the carpet and walked over to the table. There were matches and candles on the table waiting for this moment. He lit the match and the entire room seemed to light up. Everyone was surprised at how much light one, tiny match could give off. He lit the candle and even more light flared up. Mag got up to help him, and soon burning candles were evenly distributed around the room.

It wasn't like electric light; there was a dimness to it, that left details and sharp edges for the imagination. But it sufficed for basic living. Mag sat back down, and they resumed their family meeting. Once Katy calmed down, she said. "This is kinda nice, Mommy."

Mag didn't share her enthusiasm, but he kept his negative opinion to himself. It was best to let her think of it as a fun game. In fact, he added to it and fostered the ambience with a story from his childhood.

"I remember when I was a kid and a thunderstorm or ice storm would knock down power lines. The lights would go out just like this, and we'd make popcorn and sit around the fireplace and watch the glow of the light, the burning red and white embers, the yellow, orange and red flames licking up the sides of the logs."

Karen looked over at him and smiled. "That's beautiful, honey. Like something you'd write in one of your books."

He smiled back at her. "Well, I guess my writing days are over now. There's no one else to buy my books, and no time to write even if there was." He let his head drop down just a little. Cypress sensed his father's sadness and broke into the conversation.

"I think you should still write, Dad. I love reading your books. We can print them out and read them together at night just like this."

Michael nodded. "We love it when you read to us, Dad. You should keep writing."

Mag was sitting on the carpet like he always did, resting his butt on the floor and leaning back against the rocking chair between his wife's knees. She reached down and scratched his neck. "Yes, honey. I think you need to keep writing. It's who you are and it's what you do." And then she paused. "Think about it this way, people a hundred years from now will still need stories of hope and faith and light even if they still don't have electricity."

Mag thought about it for a moment. He realized she was right and added a thought of his own. "Maybe they'll need stories of hope and faith and light more than ever before." Mag ran his fingers through his hair. "Tomorrow I'll start writing the story of our family. We're very lucky you know."

There was an awkward silence. Then his brother broke in. "I found a box of twinkies today when we cleaned out the Clyborg's house."

Karen tried not to laugh, but didn't quite manage to completely stifle herself. "That's great, Johnny. Did you eat them all on the spot?"

He smiled slyly at her in the dim light. "Wait here." He got up from the couch and walked out the front door. A few minutes later he walked back in with a brown, paper bag. He sat back on the couch and opened it up. He pulled out the box of Hostess Twinkies and opened up the box. Each yellow cake was wrapped in cellophane. He took out one and passed the box on to Michael. Michael took the box but hesitated. His mom hated it when any of them ate junk food. Michael glanced over at his mother and made eye contact. She hesitated. On the one hand, she'd always insisted that her family eat nothing but healthy, clean food, but ... she knew how much those silly snack cakes meant to her brother-in-law. Perhaps some things were more important than clean food. Her mind was made up when she felt Mag gently caress her right ankle. She sighed and nodded gently to Michael. Michael smiled and took a yellow, cellophane-wrapped cake and passed it on to Mary. She smiled and took one as well. Next came Cypress and then Mag, then Katy, and last in line was Karen. She looked at the box, It was almost empty now. She looked over at Johnny. "Are you sure you want to share these?"

Johnny smiled and nodded. "It's just a Twinkie, and you guys are my family. I need to share."

Karen smiled and took out a snack cake before passing the box back over to Johnny. She resisted the motherly urge to read the ingredients label before eating it. Together, everyone unwrapped their Twinkie. But then Johnny did something unexpected. He bowed his head and prayed. Johnny was not a religious man.

"Dear God. We thank you for these Twinkies, golden, yellow sponge cake with cream filling. Individually wrapped for prolonged freshness. We thank you God for the immense sugar rush we are bout to feel. Amen."

Karen shook her head from side to side and wondered quietly, in the chaos of her own mind *How much of this can I take?* But she smiled and forced herself to take a bite. She was surprised at how good it tasted. Mag was the first to speak as they ate.

"Hey, Johnny, do you remember the first day of kindergarten for you?"

Johnny smiled in the dim light. He nodded in fond remembrance. "Oh, boy do I ever. It was my very first Twinkie!"

Mag laughed out loud. "Yeah, and it was the funniest thing I ever saw. We were late for the bus and for some reason Mom hadn't made us anything to eat. The bus was coming down the road and she had about 30 seconds to feed us both. She handed us a box of Twinkies and said, "Just don't tell yer father about this.""

Johnny laughed too and so did the kids. The laughter was infectious, and soon, Karen was smiling as well.

"Mom took that first Twinkie and shoved it into your mouth clean back to your throat and you almost choked to death."

A fond look of memory passed over Johnny's face, like he was back in time and reliving the moment.

"Yeah, bro. I remember that first Twinkie. It was the beginning of a beautiful friendship." And then his eyes misted over. "I think it was even better than ..."

Karen immediately cut him off by loudly clearing her throat. "Johnny!" She pointed with her eyes down at Katy on her lap. But Katy spurred him on.

"Better than what, Uncle Johnny?"

Johnny thought for a moment. "Well Katy, I think it was even better than the time I kissed Cassandra Harris on the playground in the third grade."

Mag nodded. "Wow! That good, huh?"

Karen smacked him on the top of his head playfully. "You'd better not have kissed Cassandra Harris on the playground, Mag!"

The children all laughed out loud. Mag kept the moment alive. "Oh, now, honey. I would never kiss and tell. Chivalry is not dead in the Jacobs clan." He paused. "But I do remember the first time I kissed you." Karen rapped him atop the head again, this time a little harder.

"Not in front of the kids, Mag!"

"Aw, honey, it was just an innocent, little kiss." And then he looked over at Michael, and saw his introspective look. And it occurred to Mag that his oldest son might be struggling with the opposite sex right now, or, more particularly, the lack of the opposite sex. Who would he marry? How would he raise a family of his own without a mate? Those were all questions that must be bouncing around inside his son's young mind. He made a mental note to talk to him about it later.

But then Katy broached the subject unexpectedly. "Daddy. If all the boys are dead, then who are Mary and I going to marry?"

The question hit him like a Mack truck and he panicked. He hadn't expected to have to answer that question, and he just wasn't prepared to deal with it right now. Lately he'd been more preoccupied with things like 'how will we get food, or how will we heat the house in the winter, or, how will we defend ourselves from people who want to hurt us. Mag waited, hoping his wife would field the question. But Karen remained silent. Both parents were surprised when Michael spoke up.

"It's nothing we need to worry about, Katy. Because God has it all planned out. The man you're going to fall in love with is already born, and God is raising him and protecting him so that he'll be ready for you when you grow up."

There was silence all around the room. It was at that moment when Mag realized how well he and Karen were doing at raising their children. At that moment he was proud of his son, more proud than he'd ever been before.

Karen reached down and rubbed the back of Mag's neck, and he gently rubbed her calf.

The apocalypse. It was here. And there were many bad things about it. Today they'd buried two more of their neighbors. They were surrounded by death, but ... they were also surrounded by life. And he thought to himself. Maybe the secret of surviving the apocalypse is to focus on the good; endure the bad, but focus like a laser on the good. Look to the light, Because the light will never fail you.

Mag broke the silence. "Good point, Michael." Then he changed the subject. "It's bed time now. Who's got first watch?"

The Jacobs family all got up and brushed their teeth and flossed, this time without running water. But, through it all, they were happy. And they smiled.

WHAT IS A TWINKIE?

Twinkies is a registered trademark of Hostess Brands, LLC. The trademark was filed on September 12th, 1960 under serial number 72104234, registration number 0717273.

Twinkies were invented by James Dewar in the year 1930 in Schiller Park, Illinois. James was an employee of The Continental Baking Company. He noticed one day that the cream machines used to make strawberry shortcake were only used during strawberry season. The rest of the year they sat idle. In an attempt to mitigate this waste, James created the cream-filled sponge cake. Instead of filling them with strawberries, he filled them with banana cream. James got the name 'Twinkies' from a billboard he saw in St. Louis advertising 'Twinkle Toe Shoes.'

During World War 2 bananas were rationed, so Twinkies were filled with vanilla cream instead. This proved to be a popular move, and was made permanent. In the 1980s different strawberry-flavored cream was tried, but people preferred the vanilla. The fruit filling was discontinued.

In the year 2011 Twinkie sales were down 20 percent as more and more consumers flocked to healthier food. The size of Twinkies was reduced, which also reduced the calorie count. The shelf life was increased from 26 to 45 days.

In 2012 Hostess filed Chapter 11 bankruptcy. Twinkie production was shut down in America for a year before finally coming back to grocery shelves.

INGREDIENTS OF A TWINKIE

Enriched Bleached Wheat Flour [Flour, Reduced Iron, B Vitamins (Niacin, Thiamine Mononitrate (B1), Riboflavin (B2), Folic Acid)], Corn Syrup, Sugar, High Fructose Corn Syrup, Water, Partially Hydrogenated Vegetable and/or Animal Shortening (Soybean, Cottonseed and/or Canola Oil, Beef Fat), Whole Eggs, Dextrose. Contains 2% or Less of: Modified Corn Starch, Glucose, Leavenings (Sodium Acid Pyrophosphate, Baking Soda, Monocalcium Phosphate), Sweet Dairy Whey, Soy Protein Isolate, Calcium and Sodium Caseinate, Salt, Mono and Diglycerides, Polysorbate 60, Soy Lecithin, Soy Flour, Cornstarch, Cellulose Gum, Sodium Stearoyl Lactylate, Natural and Artificial Flavors, Sorbic Acid (to Retain Freshness), Yellow 5, Red 40.

There are 130 calories in each Twinkie you eat featuring 4 grams of fat, 175 mg of sodium, 14.5 grams of sugar, 2 grams of protein, and 17.5 mg of cholesterol.

> *"Finally, brothers and sisters, whatever is true, whatever is noble, whatever is right, whatever is pure, whatever is lovely, whatever is admirable—if anything is excellent or praiseworthy—think about such things.."*
>
> *Philippians 4:8 (NIV)*

CHAPTER 8

**The Silver Lining of the Apocalypse**

WHEN MAG WOKE UP THE next morning, it was already light outside. His watch had been the middle of the night, so he'd slept in later than the others. As usual, he drug his weary body into the bathroom and jumped into the shower. Warm water poured down onto his drowsy body, waking up every fiber of his 42-year-old being. He quickly soaped himself down, and was getting ready to rinse off when ... suddenly, the water stopped running. And that's when he remembered it. The power went off last night.

Just then Karen walked into the bathroom. "Why are you trying to take a shower, honey. You know the power is out, so the water pump isn't running."

Mag wiped the soap out of his eyes with the wet wash cloth before answering. "Yeah, I know. I just forgot. You know my brain isn't working until after my morning shower."

Karen laughed out loud, but tried to be supportive. "You just wait here, honey. I'll go to the hand pump and run a bucket of water so you can rinse off."

The Jacobs family had paid over 3,000 dollars to dig a second well with a hand pump. It had been a large chunk of change for someone with his wage, but one he and Karen had agreed was necessary ... just in case. The well went down over 100 feet, and the pump had been special-ordered and more expensive to buy than a regular farm pump that went down only 10 to 20 feet. It was the kind you'd see at parks and cemeteries.

Karen came in with the bucket of water and stood beside the shower curtain. "Get ready, honey. I'll just pour it over your head and you can get all the soap off you."

Mag situated himself, and Karen poured the bucket of water onto Mag's head. It seemed ice-cold to him and he screamed as loud as he could.

"Ahh, honey, it's cold! Ahh! Stop! Stop!"

Karen stopped pouring, but couldn't stop laughing. "What are you whining about, Mag. It's a perfect 53 degrees. It's straight out of the ground."

Mag regained his pride and composure. "Okay, I get it. You did that on purpose just to hear me scream."

Karen smiled. "You can't prove that."

She lifted the bucket and began pouring it on him again until the pail was empty. Mag shivered inside the shower stall while Karen walked out of the room. "Breakfast is ready, my love."

Mag cursed under his breath after she'd gone before thinking to himself, *Well, I'm definitely awake now!* Then he quickly toweled off and got dressed. At the breakfast table, they prayed and then talked while eating.

"It was weird on guard duty last night, Dad." Michael heaped some eggs onto his spoon and shoveled them into his mouth. Mag looked over at him.

"Oh Yeah? Why's that?"

"Before it was just quiet out there. No trains, planes and automobiles, but now ... you know those cell towers that are all over to the north and east of us, the ones with the blinking red lights up at the top?"

Mag nodded and Michael continued talking. "Well, they don't blink anymore. There's nothing but stars out there and the moon. I kinda like it."

And then Katy broke into the conversation. "Daddy, can Mary and I look through my telescope tonight?"

Mag glanced over at Karen and she answered for him. "I think that would be okay, Mag. We need to continue with the home schooling as best we can."

Cypress looked over at his mom in amazement. "Why in the world would we need an education now?"

His mom got a stern look on her face and answered resolutely. "Because I say so."

Cypress knew better than to argue with her, so he didn't reply. But Mag could tell by the confused looks on his boy's faces, that they needed a better answer than that.

"Honey, maybe we should reconsider what we're teaching the kids."

She stopped eating. "Why is that?"

The kids looked up from their plates, wondering if there was going to be a disagreement between their parents. And then Karen thought about it for a second.

"Do you mean we should be teaching them things that will help us survive, rather than things like computer science, banking and the stuff that they'll never use now that things have changed so much?"

Mag nodded. "Yeah. We should still have them master the basics, like reading, writing and math, history, the constitution and the Bible, but maybe we can also throw in survival skills that could mean life or death to all of us. Things like fire-starting, agriculture, food preservation, military tactics and medical skills."

Karen thought about it for a few moments. Mag just kept eating as she thought. Finally, she concurred. "Yeah, honey, that has some merit. But you'll have to help. Maybe you can handle the history and civics and military stuff."

Mag agreed while nodding his head. "Yeah, I can do that. It's not like I have a steady job anymore. Right now my only job is to gather food, supplies and make sure we can survive through the winter." And then a thought occurred to him *Maybe the colonel could help out with this?*

Mary seldom talked, but she raised her hand and Karen smiled. "Yes, sweety, what is it?"

"Well, I was wondrin' if Katy and I could help with getting food and stuff."

Karen smiled and nodded her head. "Absolutely, honey. I was hoping you and Katy could help me finish canning the meat today. Would you like that?"

Mary and Katy both beamed. Then Karen turned back to her husband. "So, what are you and the boys doing today?"

And then Mag changed the subject. "Where's my brother?"

"I don't know. He never came in this morning. Maybe he's still sleeping."

Michael laughed. "I saw him eat the rest of that box of Twinkies last night. Maybe he slipped into a sugar coma."

And then Mag answered his wife's original question. "Cypress will be training with the colonel this morning on the short wave. I worked it out with him last time I was over there. Michael and I are going to the surrounding farms to check on livestock."

Karen finished eating and got up to clear the table. Everyone else helped. The boys brought in several 5-gallon buckets of water from the pump so Karen and the girls could do the dishes. Cypress took his bike over to the colonel's house, and Michael and Mag went out to check on Johnny.

"Michael, where's my truck?"

Just then, they heard the roar of the engine as it approached from the southwest. A few seconds later Johnny pulled to a stop in the paved driveway. He was grinning from ear to ear.

"You'll never guess what I found, Mag!"

Mag walked over to the pick-up and looked into the bed. "I think you found 12 propane tanks for our barbecue grill."

Johnny turned his head to the bed of the truck. "Well, yeah, I did find those. I thought Karen could can the meat faster if she used the grill. It runs hotter and faster than the gas stove in the kitchen." He laughed out loud. Then he picked up a pair of bolt cutters from the bottom of the truck bed and held them up for him to see. "They were on sale, so I just bought them all."

Michael smiled. He liked his Uncle Johnny's sense of humor. "I'll help you unload them, Uncle Johnny."

After they were all loaded into the pole barn, they stood in front of the overhead door and talked.

"Did you see anyone while you were in town."

Johnny shook his head from side to side, then he ran his left hand through his graying hair. He and Mag looked a lot alike, same height and build, but Mag's hair was still light brown, graying only at the temples.

"I saw Jerry, but he doesn't talk much when he's passed out on the pavement. I feel sorry for that guy." And then he got an introspective look on his face that Mag wasn't used to. "Ya know, Mag, that could've been me if this whole apocalypse thing hadn't happened."

Mag looked over at his brother and made eye contact. Michael just stood by silently and listened to the two men.

"What do you mean?"

He turned away as if in shame. "I was working on a first-class drinking problem, bro. I know Karen doesn't like that and all, and I came over here a few times drunk, but ... " His words trailed off into the morning. "This is gonna sound kinda funny, but ... I feel more alive now than I have since you and I were kids."

Mag thought about it. "How so?"

"Well, just look at me. I haven't had a drink since the night before the big bombs started falling. To be honest with you, I haven't even thought about it."

Mag didn't say anything, so Michael asked. "So why exactly did you drink so much before?"

Johnny laughed. "I don't know for sure, but ... I think I was just bored outta my skull. I had no purpose. Nothing worthwhile to do. I was jumpin' from one woman to the next just for fun, and I just got caught up in a lifestyle that was all about making myself feel good. And I know that's against my upbringing and all, so it made me feel guilty. But when I drank, the guilt got dimmer." He hesitated, wondering if he should even say the next words. "I think, Mag. I think maybe the end of the world saved my life."

Mag smiled at his little brother and then reached over and squeezed his left shoulder with his right hand. Mag was reminded of his thoughts while on the rubber raft, drifting across Lake Michigan. He'd had to force himself to stay positive, to keep thinking about all the good things in his life that he was fighting to get back to.

"I can understand that."

The whole while Mag and his brother were talking to each other, Michael just listened and took it all in. Truth be told he was more than a little bit angry about the apocalypse. He was a young man, not even fully grown. He was ambitious, with his whole life ahead of him. He'd made plans and commitments to himself about what he'd do, where he'd go, things he'd build and conquer and ... but they were all gone now. His life had imploded in on itself without any warning or discussion. Mag should have noticed his son's mood, but he didn't. He was too focused on his brother.

And then the tender moment was gone, like a candle that had just been blown out by a stiff, western wind.

"Can you stay here while Michael and I head over to the Vandenberg farm and check out the situation there?"

Johnny nodded and headed off to the kitchen to check on the meat canning. Mag tossed his son the truck keys and hopped into the passenger seat with his AR-15 pointed toward the ceiling.

CANNING MEAT

There are a lot of different ways to preserve food during the apocalypse. Drying. fermenting and salting food has been around since the beginning of recorded history, so far as we know. But food canning is a relatively recent development that first took place in the late 18th century.

Napoleon Bonaparte, the famous French dictator, needed a way to feed his army as it marched across Europe on it conquesting campaign, so he offered a reward in 1795 to anyone who could come up with a way to feed his military. A man named Nicholas Appert came up with the idea of heat-processing the food in glass jars that were reinforced with wire. He would then seal the glass jars of food with wax.

I recall my mother doing this with her jellies and jams when I was a kid. We always had a terrible time getting the wax off the top, and we were always eating tiny chunks of paraffin in our peanut butter and jelly sandwiches.

Then in 1810 an Englishman named Peter Durand created a way to seal food in unbreakable tin cans, however, the method wasn't used commercially until the year 1912. It's ironic that people knew that spoiled food could kill you, and that canned food was safe; they just had no idea why it worked until Louis Pasteur discovered how microorganisms made food to spoil and cause disease.

John Mason invented the threaded metal rings with lids and rubber seals back in 1858. Leaders in the industry were William Charles Ball and Alexander Kerr.

WHY DID THE GAS RANGE STILL WORK?

While all electric ranges were rendered impotent and useless for the duration of the power-grid failure, Karen still was able to use her gas stove to cook and to can meat. Why was that? Well, a normal gas range doesn't run on electricity. It runs on either liquid propane or natural gas. The Jacobs family has a large, 500-gallon tank of propane in their back yard. Country people sometimes call it a "pig" because of it's fat, oblong shape. The gas range will function just fine for as long as there is propane inside the tank. But once it runs out, it will cease to function.

Of course, modern gas ranges have certain functions that run on electricity, like the clock, the timer and anything with programming. But the gas will flow and burn just fine.

Most modern ranges have an electronic ignition system, just like your barbecue grill that gives off a little spark which ignites the gas. From now on, the Jacobs will have to ignite the gas with a match, candle, lighter or some other source of open flame. Be careful never to turn on the gas and let it pour into the house. People have blown up their houses that way.

> *"I have no need of a bull from your stall or of goats from your pens, for every animal of the forest is mine, and the cattle on a thousand hills."*
>
> *Psalm 50:9-10 (NIV)*

CHAPTER 9

The Vandenberg Farm

MICHAEL AND MAG SMELLED the Vandenberg farm long before they pulled into the gravel driveway.

"Dad, can you believe that smell? What is it?"

Michael pulled to a stop out by the pole barn where he knew Bob Vandenberg stored his combines. "That's cow manure, son."

"But why is it so strong today?"

Mag thought about it before answering. "I suppose the stalls haven't been cleaned out in a long time."

Michael looked over at his father apprehensively. Michael was friends with one of the Vandenberg sons, not close friends, but they'd played little league baseball together a few years back, and Michael had secretly hoped the boy was still alive. He'd also had a crush on their daughter for much of his teen years, though he'd never told anyone about it.

Michael shut off the engine and listened. There were cows bawling in the background, and a rooster crowed incessantly behind the farm house. Mag rolled down the window and sniffed again. Michael did the same.

"I don't smell any dead bodies, Dad. That's a good sign."

His father nodded. "Yes, I agree. Maybe they're all still alive."

Michael smiled. He needed some good news today. Michael started to get out, but Mag put his left arm on his son's arm to stop him. "Not yet, son. Let's leave our carbines locked up in the truck. If they're still alive, they might be a little on edge."

Michael agreed and both men propped their AR-15s up against the seat before getting out. Michael pressed the key fob to lock the door behind them. They both started walking carefully toward the house. Both their pistols were concealed beneath flannel so as not to pose a threat to the Vandenberg's.

"Do you smell that, Dad?"

Mag stopped walking, and his son followed suit. "Yeah. What is that?"

Michael looked up at the side door of the house. The kitchen window was open. "That's a good smell, Dad."

Indeed it was. "It smells like apple pie." Mag smiled and started walking again. The Vandenbergs had two sons, the oldest was 23, then Tim at 16. They had a daughter, age 19 who'd just left again for college this fall. Mag and Michael took a few more steps and then froze in their tracks when they heard the racking sound of a pump shotgun.

"That's far enough. Don't move and don't go for those guns under your shirts."

Mag and Michael slowly put up their hands. Mag waited a few seconds, then started to turn toward the voice. "Don't move! Don't turn! You make one more move and I'll blast you in the back."

Mag stopped. He had no doubt the man would carry through with his threat, and he had no wish to be killed or wounded with double aught buckshot.

"You're not Bob Vandenberg. What have you done with him?"

The man didn't mince words. "I'll be asking the questions around here. "Who are you?"

"My name's Mag Jacobs; this is my son. Michael. We're friends with Bob and Marie. We go to church with them."

There was a silence, as if the man was processing Mag's words. A sudden breeze kicked up and a shiver ran down Mag's spine. This was the second time in just a few days he'd been held at gun point.

"Well, maybe you are and maybe you aren't." And then the man yelled as loud as he could.

"Bob! I got two guys out here at gun point say they know you. I could use some help."

It was an agonizing 30 seconds as they waited for a response. Bob Vandenberg turned the corner with a double-barrelled shotgun in his hands. When he saw Mag and Michael, he smiled.

"Put the gun down, brother. These are friends."

The man with the shotgun looked apprehensively over at Bob, before finally lowering the gun to point back at the ground. "You sure, Bob?"

Bob didn't answer. He lowered his own shotgun and walked out into the open toward them. When he reached Mag, he extended his right hand. Mag took it and squeezed firmly.

"Bob, it's good to see you alive. We haven't seen anyone alive since the bombs fell." And then he added, "Well, other than Jerry over at the dollar store. I doubt he'll be alive much longer at the rate he's drinking though."

Bob frowned. He was a tall man, like most of the Dutch farmers in the area. He was about 45 years old, and well over 6 feet in height. His blonde hair was graying on the sides.

"That's a sad thing. I always felt sorry for that guy."

Then he turned to Michael and extended his hand in friendship. Michael turned to his father who immediately nodded. Bob saw the interaction and smiled again.

"It's okay, Mag. None of us came up sick. Don't know why, but we're all healthy here. Just the mercy of God I suppose."

Michael shook his hand. He hadn't done that in a long time, and it felt oddly reassuring.

"Is Tim okay?"

The tall man nodded. "You bet. He's in the pole barn working on one of the tractors. Head on up there, but announce yourself before walking in. He's packing and a little tense right now. He had to shoot a man last week."

Michael walked away, just as the stranger walked up and stood beside Bob. "Mag, I'd like you to meet my older brother, Harold. He and his family came up from Illinois before everything went to hell in a hand basket."

The man looked a lot like his brother. The Dutch heritage was a strong gene. Harold put out his hand. He was obviously about 5 years older than his brother. Mag accepted it and smiled as best he could.

"I'm sorry about the shotgun and all. I didn't know you."

Mag nodded. "I understand. It's a different world now, and you just can't be too careful these days."

"You got that right." Then Bob started to walk back toward the house and waved for him to follow. "Come on up to the house for some coffee. I know Marie will be happy to see a friendly face again. She's been going crazy in there not knowing."

"Bob, I'm going to help Tim with the tractor while you two talk." Bob nodded as his brother walked away toward the pole barn. Once inside the kitchen, Marie threw her arms around Mag and cried. Then she bombarded him with question after question.

"Is Karen okay? What about the kids? Is there anyone else alive that you know of?"

Mag patiently answered each of her questions one at a time as she asked them. It was so good to see another person, one he knew and trusted, one who cared about himself and his family.

As she talked, Marie poured both Mag and her husband a cup of coffee. She looked down at the old-fashioned per-colator and laughed. "I almost threw this old thing out a million times in the past 20 years, but it belonged to Bob's mom, so I just couldn't bring myself to do it. I'm so glad now that I kept it."

Mag blew on his coffee before taking a tiny sip. They didn't have a percolator, so Karen was boiling water with coffee in it, then straining out the grounds. Inevitably, a few of the grounds made it through the process, and he'd have to pick them out of his teeth. But this coffee was beautiful.

"Tell me, Marie. Did I smell one of your world-famous apple pies while I was walking up the drive?"

Just then another woman in her late forties walked into

the kitchen. She looked surprised and perhaps even a bit frightened when she saw Mag. No one spoke at first, so she just stood there. Finally, she said.

"Oh, Hi. I'm Harold's wife, Sara."

Mag smiled and stood up out of respect. "It's a pleasure to meet you, Sara. I've already met your husband."

Bob laughed. "He sure did! At the end of a shotgun!"

Marie was the first to speak. "Oh my. Did Harold hurt you, Mag?"

Mag laughed now. "Well, no. Bob rescued me just in time. He seems like a nice guy when he's not threatening to blow you away."

Sara looked down in shame. "I'm so sorry, Mag. He just hasn't been himself since all this Covid stuff started happening, and then there were the bombs, and now no electricity. He's been a little uptight lately."

And then she turned to Marie. "Can I cut him a slice of apple pie, dear, to make it up to him. Marie smiled and nodded. "Of course, Sara. It's the least we can do after almost killing our best neighbor." And then Mag thought to himself *I might be their only neighbor.*

A few minutes later, Mag looked down at the large slice of hot apple pie. His mouth was watering so fast he could hardly hold the reflex in check. He lifted the first fork-full to his lips and placed it on his tongue. He closed his mouth and savored it like nourishment to a starving man.

"Oh, Marie, This is the best. Thank you so much."

She watched and talked while Mag ate. Bob didn't say much, but his wife talked so long and fast that he couldn't have talked even if he'd wanted to. Sara, the sister-in-law, sat down at the red, formica-topped kitchen table and just listened quietly as well.

Mag told them about his harrowing trip to the upper peninsula, the successful book tour, then his trip floating almost to Wisconsin on Lake Michigan in a rubber raft. Then he told them about the shoot-out over by Hopkins, then the altercation with Jerry at the dollar store, and about Mary and her dead parents. He also told them all he'd learned from the colonel about how the virus infected people; it's incubation period, and the staggering death toll.

And then Mag asked them a question. "Do you know anyone else who is alive?"

Bob and Marie both grew silent. Finally, Bob was the first to speak. "Our cell phones went dead a while back. We haven't heard from anyone since last week. You're the first live person we've seen since this all went down."

And then something occurred to Mag. "What about your daughter, Abby? Didn't she just head off to college again a few weeks ago?"

Bob looked over at his wife who started to cry. Mag felt like an idiot. "I'm sorry." And then he paused. "When was the last time you heard from her?"

Bob fielded the question for his crying wife. "It was the day after that bomb fell on Chicago. She called us from her dorm room. Said most of the students were getting sick and some were dying. We told her to come straight home, and she tried. But her car broke down and she walked back to the college. The last we heard was a text that said she'd wait it out there at the dorm until we could come get her."

Mag thought about it. He knew what he'd do if his kid was stuck somewhere during all this. He'd move mountains and risk anything to get to them. He wanted to discuss this with Karen before making the offer, but ... come to think of it he didn't need to. Mag knew exactly what his wife would say.

"So when are you going to get her?"

There was a deafening silence.

"Have you already tried to get her?"

The silence grew even louder.

"Where did she go to college? Wasn't it in Grand Rapids somewhere?"

Bob finally answered. "Yeah. She went to Cornerstone down on the East Beltline. Tim and I went there the following day and almost got killed. We didn't even make it to the college. As soon as we reached 68th street we got hit by a gang of kids. "I call them kids, but they all had guns and they shot up our truck. They chased us a few miles before our truck overheated. Then we had to pull over and run. They chased us and we shot two of them before they backed off."

Mag nodded and moved his elbows up onto the table where he placed his chin atop his fists.

"I see."

Bob continued. "It took us three days to walk back home. No one would stop and give us a ride. I thought about stealing a car, but ... I just couldn't bring myself to do it. If I had to do it over again, though ... I think I would."

Mag reached down and picked up his coffee cup. It was cool enough that he didn't have to blow off steam. He took a sip and set it back down.

"What kind of guns did you have?"

Bob lowered his head. "Just the two shotguns we use for hunting. Those are the only guns we've got."

Mag smiled softly. "Not anymore."

Bob looked at him quizzically. Marie suddenly stopped

crying, her eyes full of hope.

"I want you to come on over to my house this afternoon. We'll meet with the colonel and come up with a rescue plan." He smiled. "We're going to get your little girl, Bob. I promise you that."

They talked a few more minutes, then Mag got up and said his good byes. He went back out to the truck, gathered up his boy and drove home. Then he walked over to see Buzz. Suddenly, there was a lot more work to do.

DOMESTIC LIVESTOCK

AND THE APOCALYPSE

The American farming industry is based on petroleum, electricity and computer-based technology. Without petroleum, farmers would not be able to plow their fields, spray pesticides, scatter fertilizer, and plant and harvest their crops.

Nine-tenths of the livestock in our story would die within a few weeks, simply because the people who normally feed and water them are now dead. The era of small, family-owned farms in America is almost over. Most farms are now run by large corporations. They are highly mechanized and scientifically operated. Once the electricity goes off, these mega farms will be untended. A single farm can house thousands of animals. Most of the cows are in stalls. They will die within a few days and begin to rot. The same will happen with egg farms, poultry farms and pig farms. Some of the animals may be able to escape their pens and become feral, but there is no guarantee of that.

Domesticated livestock like cows and chickens are not bred and prepared to survive in the wild. They will be eaten by predators, mostly coyotes, wild dogs and wolves that will spread down from the north. Pigs and goats may fare better, simply because they are omnivores, meaning they'll eat just about anything.

THE SHOTGUN LIMITATION

The common shotgun is an awesome tool for home defense, especially against home invasions in the modern world. Its big strength is knock-down power. A 12-gauge shotgun with double-aught buckshot will deliver roughly 1,200 plus feet per second of muzzle velocity as well as 1,500 plus foot-pounds of energy. The combined weight of nine double-aught buckshot pellets is 484 grains. Each pellet is roughly a third of an inch in diameter, and there are 9 pellets per round.

When used inside your home for defense, these rounds are deadly and have a lot of advantages, but for longer range defense, more similar to open-air combat situations, you'd be better off with a battle rifle or carbine with a much longer range and 30-round magazine capacity.

Now, don't get me wrong, I have a shotgun in my bedroom for home defense, but, during the apocalypse when battles are likely to occur outside the home and against multiple assailants, I'll take my AR-15 type carbine or AK-47. Shotguns are great when going room to room and clearing at short distances, but when the distance is measured in yards instead of feet, then trade in the shotgun for the carbine or rifle. Better yet ... get two or three of each!

But the Lord said to Gideon, "There are still too many men. Take them down to the water, and I will thin them out for you there. If I say, 'This one shall go with you,' he shall go; but if I say, 'This one shall not go with you,' he shall not go.".

Judges 7:4 (NIV)

CHAPTER 10

__Cornerstone University, Grand Rapids, MI__

THE PEOPLE HAD DIED SO SUD-
denly, that no one had taken the time to lock
the doors before going home. Cornerstone
was a small college to be sure, with a friendly, close-
knit community of believers, almost like an extension of
Abby's family, and that was the biggest reason she'd put
off leaving for home as long as she had.

She was a sophomore this year, and had so many
friends, friends that needed her, that had asked her to stay
for just a little while longer. And, to her own regret, she'd
done just that. Abby still remembered the dead and dying all around her, lying on their beds or couches in the
common room. She was planning on going into medical
school, so she'd felt a natural desire to stay and nurse as
many people back to health as possible. She'd thought of
it as the Christian thing to do; to lay down her own life
for her friends. But, oddly enough, that hadn't happened.

Abby had never died, but all of her friends had. And now she was living among the stench of their dead and decaying bodies. Most of them were in the dorm rooms, so she'd moved out of there day before yesterday, and now was living in the Hansen Athletic Center.

Fortunately, she had the keys to the building and most other buildings for the campus. Getting the keys had been very traumatic for her. The security guard had been dead for several days by the time she'd found him. His body had been bloated up and smelly. Abby had rolled him over with a mop handle and frisked him from top to bottom before finding what she'd needed. She'd felt terrible doing it, like somehow she was violating some sacred trust or respect for the dead. But she'd had bigger problems than obeying old mores that no longer worked.

There had been only a few dead bodies in the Hanson Athletic Center, and she was now living in the lower level in a sports equipment room just off the basketball court. There was a smaller room within and she could lock herself inside for extra security. She needed that especially while she slept, simply because every so often looters would come and look for food or other things to steal.

Just the day before a man had tried to trap her on the main floor while she'd been raiding a vending machine. Abby had broken through the plastic using a javelin from the sports equipment room and pilfered some Gatorade and crackers to keep from starving to death. The man had come up behind her and wrapped his arms around her chest in a bear hug. With a strength she hadn't known she possessed, she'd fought back, throwing her head back as far as she could, and smashing into the man's nose. She'd turned around to see the blood dripping out, and the look of surprise and then anger as he came toward her again.

Abby had raised up the javelin and propped it against the face of the metal vending machine. The man ran into it, and shoved the spear into his chest far enough to hit his heart. Abby remembered the look of shock on the man's face as he quickly bled out on the end of the javelin.

It had taken her five minutes to pull out the metal spear, and she'd had to wiggle it around to loosen it from the man's chest cavity. But, in the end, she'd gotten back her weapon as well as all the snacks.

Abby was laying on the padded floor mat now, looking at the darkness of the room. The power had gone out, and there were no windows inside. She didn't even know what time it was. Her cell phone had died a few days ago, and she had no way to recharge it. Deep inside her soul, she still struggled with what she'd done. She thought to herself *I killed a man!* That was a thought and regret she'd never dreamed of having before all this bad stuff had cut loose.

She'd prayed to God, right here on this mat, begging his forgiveness, but ... she just didn't feel his grace, at least not yet. Perhaps the feelings of forgiveness would come later. In her head it was easy to justify it, because it had been him or her, but ... it was just a tough thing to deal with, something she wasn't prepared morally or emotionally to reconcile.

One thing that really bothered her even more than that was her family. They hadn't come for her. And she couldn't help but wonder ... *are they still alive*? She unscrewed the cap to the Gatorade and took another drink. She was starting to loathe Gatorade, even though it was all that was keeping her alive.

Abby had no outside information. She'd found a battery powered radio, but got nothing but static. Her parents, her brothers, they could all be dead. And, if they were still alive, why hadn't they come for her?

A plan had been hatching in her mind over the past two days of thinking, and she'd went to God in prayer about it. What if she could steal one of the cars in the student parking lot. All she had to do was go back to the dorm rooms and search for keys. If she could find some keys and match it with the right car, then she could be home within an hour.

But every time she thought about it her conscious flared up, preventing her from carrying through with the plan. She just couldn't bring herself to steal something, even if the owners were already dead. And then she thought to herself *maybe I'm just not cut out for the end of the world*. And she wondered ... *am I going to die right here, on this campus filled with death, inside a tomb of once-friends and classmates*.

She bowed her head and asked God for guidance, but He said nothing. She cried out loud in the darkness, giving in to momentary despair before finally falling back to sleep.

The Jacobs Home

MICHAEL JACOBS SAT AROUND THE TABLE WITH HIS father, Bob Vandenberg and the colonel. They were drinking coffee. Michael didn't like coffee, but it seemed the thing for men to do, so he forced himself to swallow the bitter drink. His mother came up behind him and put her hand on his neck. Just a few weeks ago that wouldn't have bothered him, but now ... something was different. He had to forcibly stop himself from pushing her away. He knew she loved him, would die for him, but ... something about it embarrassed him. He focused back on what the colonel was saying.

"What we need here is a rapid-response team. We get in fast, with sufficient force and firepower, and then we get back out again before superior forces can come to bear."

"How many are you thinking about, Buzz?"

The colonel looked over at Mag before responding. "Just four of the people at this table."

Michael felt his mother's hand tighten around his neck. He prayed she wouldn't say anything, but she did.

"Why Michael? He's so young?"

Buzz looked up at her and frowned. While he understood her protest, had indeed anticipated it; he couldn't let it stand. "Because I trust my life to him. Because he's battle-hardened and tested in combat. He knows how to shoot, and he's a good fighter." He waited, but Karen said nothing. "He's already saved the lives of two men at this table, Karen. I know he's only 16, but how many men has he already killed in combat? He has more battle time than most soldiers twice his age. If he doesn't go, then it decreases our chance for success. We'll have to take someone less skilled and less qualified." His face hardened up as he spoke. "And I don't know about you, Mrs. Jacobs, but I'd like to come back here and finish out my retirement."

There was nothing but silence around the room. Finally, Michael felt his mother's hand loosen and then fall away altogether. She quietly left the room.

Mag wondered if he should go after her, but decided against it. Best to let her think about this for a while before taking her on. The truth was, he didn't want to take Michael either, but ... he knew in his head that everything the colonel had said was true. His son was a battle-hardened soldier now, and he'd be a real asset to the strike force. He kept quiet and listened as the colonel laid out the plan.

AFTER THE MEETING, MICHAEL SOUGHT OUT HIS mother. He found her on the porch swing on the front deck. He walked up and sat down beside her. She ignored his presence; it was a coldness that he'd never felt from her before.

Michael didn't have a script, didn't know what was best to say, so he just spoke from his heart. "I'll come back, Mom, I promise you I will." She said nothing. "You know how much I love you. You're my mom and I love you."

The sun was just beginning to set in the west. They both watched it silently for several minutes. Finally she spoke to him.

"I don't think I could bear to live without you, honey." Michael dropped his head down and sighed. "I know what you mean. I feel the same way, but ..." And then he told her something that he'd never told anyone else before.

"I've had a terrible crush on Abby ever since I was in the third grade."

That seemed to affect his mother. Karen turned from the sun and looked him in the eyes. "Are you serious?"

Michael nodded."Yeah, I know she's older than me, but ... she's just so pretty and so nice. She was always nice to me, Mom, even though I'm just a kid to her."

Karen collapsed back into the wood of the porch swing. She let her back hit it harder than she wanted. "Wow! I wasn't expecting that one."

Her son smiled softly. "I'm not saying I'll marry her, but ..." He looked back at the setting sun. "I don't know what I'm saying. I just have feelings for her and I couldn't live with myself if she was still alive and I didn't go and get her."

Karen leaned her left shoulder into her son and then put her arm around him. "You are so like your father."

"That's good, right?"

She laughed just a tad. "Yeah, that's a good thing. That man has more love for me than anyone ever could. Your father would crawl over busted glass to save me. He'd walk through fire. He'd ..." She hesitated. "You're a man now, Michael, and you have to do what you think is best." A tear rolled down her cheek. "I'll support you the same as I would your father. If you think it's right then you should go."

A great heaviness lifted off Michael's heart, and he loved his mother more than ever before. He reached over and gave her a hug and a squeeze.

"Thanks Mom. I'll be careful, and I'll come back. I promise you I will."

She moved her right hand over and grabbed onto his chin and lifted it toward her. "You'd better son." And then she hesitated. "And bring your father home with you."

THE NEXT TWO HOURS WERE SPENT GOING OVER THE plan and loading up supplies. Mag took an hour to drill Bob in the proper use of the AR-15 he'd given him. Then they went behind the house to his private range and shot about 60 rounds just to make sure he understood the sighting system. Bob had never used night vision before, but he caught on real fast.

They loaded the supplies into the bed of the truck and then met on the front porch to say good bye. Mag pulled Karen off to one side and spoke to her gently.

"Honey, I'm very proud of you. I know you don't un-derstand us men, but I can tell you that you've earned the respect of your son for the rest of his life."

She gave him a disdainful look. "I think I understand you better than you think, Mag Jacobs." And then she thought about all the mean, angry things she wanted to say to him, but ... then she let them slide on by into the fading sunset. "Just promise me you'll look after him. I could lose both my men in this one fight to rescue a girl who didn't have enough sense to come home when she should have. I'm not happy with her."

That statement took Mag by surprise, and he was sure there was something more to it that he didn't know but he let it go for now. He held her against his chest and whis-pered into her ear."I love you sweetheart, and you know I'll come back even if I have to kill every single bad guy between here and Grand Rapids."

Finally, she relented and hugged him back. "Just make sure you bring our son back with you. That's all I'm ask-ing."

He kissed her and they separated. Mag went over to Cypress and Johnny to give them last-minute instructions on protecting the family while he was gone. Of course, Cypress had wanted to go too, but the immediate and ir-revocable answer had been no. Besides, there was always the chance that they wouldn't make it back, and, if that happened, Karen would need him more than ever.

Mag went over to Katy and Mary and dropped down to one knee on the grass beside the deck. "Now you two have to take care of your mother while I'm gone. She's going to need extra help until I get back."

"So when ya gettin' back, Daddy?"

Mag hugged his little caboose, and then brought Mary

in for the group hug. "It won't be too long. We hope to be back before morning, but, it might take longer than that. So don't worry about us. Just pray for our safety, okay?"

Katy smiled and kissed him on the cheek. Mary just looked at him blankly and gave him a final hug. Then they both ran off to play.

All the while others were saying their good byes, the colonel sat shotgun in the front seat of the crew cab pick-up truck. He looked out at his men and a heaviness grew in his heart. All his life he'd sent men into battle and sometimes they'd died, but this was different. All those soldiers had had families, but he'd never seen them, talked to them, even been friends with them. This was different, more personal, and he vowed to do his best to bring them all back home.

Just as the sun was setting, they jumped into the cab and drove away into the dusky night.

THE ART OF WAR PLANNING

Mag and his rescue team have one very good advantage. It's the colonel. The colonel, unknown to even Mag, was the veteran of dozens of firefights. He'd been awarded three purple Hearts, two silver stars and the Distinguished Service Cross.

Aside from that, he'd served for several years as a war planner. In short, Colonel Buzz knew how to fight a battle, and he almost always won. His planning and quick-reaction skills were to prove decisive over the next few hours.

While Mag had seen combat, as had Michael, it wasn't on par with the colonel's experience. They were both good fighters, level-headed under stress, but they didn't have the experience making the hard decisions in a second's notice while under fire.

In short, this pending battle was lesser than many of the colonel's previous military challenges, but with only four men, so much could go wrong. And their intel was sketchy at best.

No matter how good his skills, it was still possible they'd all die in the coming battle.

THE PAIN OF LEADERSHIP

One of my favorite movies is *Gettysburg*, with Martin Sheen as Robert E. Lee and Tom Beringer as General Longstreet. On the eve of battle, General Lee makes this statement to General Longstreet:

> *"To be a good soldier, you must love the army. To be a good commander, you must be willing to order the death of the thing you love."*

One advantage Buzz has over Mag is this: Mag could never order the death of his son in combat, even if he knew it was best. He'd be willing to sacrifice the mission to save his son. That is natural and good, but not for a commander in battle.

However, the colonel is not clouded by familial love. He loves his soldiers, but loves the smell of battle and victory even more.

> *"During the night Abram divided his men to attack them and he routed them, pursuing them as far as Hobah, north of Damascus."*
>
> *Genesis 14:15 (NIV)*

CHAPTER 11

The Road to Rescue

THEY WERE DRIVING DOWN Patterson Road, and they'd just passed M179 on the way to Grand Rapids; the locals called it Chief Noonday Road. Patterson was just a two-lane road running through farmland between the city and Gun Lake, a vacation and resort community. The colonel had selected this route simply because it was rural and less likely to be patrolled by highwaymen. Buzz had spent the past few days monitoring local ham radio and was aware of roving bands of criminals who pretty much took what they wanted with impunity. The anarchy was a dream come true for anyone with criminal inclination, so they kept alert on the drive in.

Mag watched the sides of the road for deer as he drove. The last thing they needed to do was hit one of them and have to walk all the way back home before day light. He thought about the changes of the last 2 weeks and was amazed. Two weeks ago hitting a deer with your car would be a nuisance and might cost you some money for car repairs, but now ... it could cost you your life.

They saw a few houses with dim lights inside and chimneys with smoke rising out the stack, silhouetted against the light of the full moon. Once they passed 84th street, Mag pulled over. No one said anything; there was nothing to say. It was a plan, and all they had to do was carry it out. Mag turned off the headlights and the running lights and quickly donned the night vision goggles they'd gotten from Brody Connor's house.

Within two minutes he was on the road again, and tooling along at 70 miles per hour. He didn't stop for signs, and the traffic lights just hung like dead ghosts, suspended over the road crossings. Mag couldn't help but second guess the wisdom of what they were doing. Bob Vandenberg was a friend, but ... he was putting his whole family in jeopardy. Still ... he believed in the golden rule, and this is what he'd want Bob to do for him should the roles be reversed. Everything about the apocalypse upped the ante; every decision, every misstep, any tiny mistake could result in death at the next turn.

They reached the East Beltline and turned left, then a quick right to stay on Patterson. A few miles down they passed the Gerald Ford International Airport. Two weeks ago it would have been a central hub of activity, but tonight it was venerable graveyard without light. Mag could see the looming hulks of powerful jetliners resting forever dead on the runways. They would never fly again.

They drove through an industrial park, flanked with once-thriving businesses on both sides of the road. They came to 28th Street and turned right to get on Interstate 96. They saw several vehicles at the Costco on the right, but they drove by unnoticed. Mag heard several gunshots but kept driving. There was a similar situation at the Meijer Superstore beside the highway, but it didn't affect them. Just as Buzz had predicted, the highway was clear of traffic, and soon Mag had the truck up to 100 miles per hour. Just a few minutes later they took the East Beltline exit and turned right toward the college. They ignored the Michigan left law and just turned onto Bradford street so they could approach from the south.

"Slow down, Mag. Run silent and don't rev the engine. The less attention we raise the better. We don't really know what we're up against here."

Mag slowed to 15 miles per hour as they coasted up to the campus. He took the first left into a small parking lot. He shut off the engine and all was silent again. They all listened to the sound of the engine as it cooled.

Finally, the colonel broke the silence. "All right, men. Let's gear up and get in position."

Hansen Athletc Center

ABBY WOKE UP AND LOOKED AROUND HER. THE equipment room was safe, but it was always so very dark, and she couldn't wait any longer to get outside again and enact her plan to return home. She found it odd that just a few weeks ago she'd seen the college as her second home, but now it was a tomb, filled with the remains of all she'd once loved. She thought of her parents and her brothers, on the farm she'd grown up on, and her church. She desperately wanted to go home.

She got up and straightened her dirty and wrinkled clothing before picking up the javelin beside her. Then she donned the book pack filled with a knife, some toilet paper and food from the vending machines. Quickly, she unlocked the door and slipped out into the hallway to the gymnasium. Slowly, she crept up one flight of stairs to the balcony overlooking the gym. She peered out into the darkness through the glass viewing panes, wishing she could see in the dark. As quietly as possible she opened the glass door and squeezed through it into the main hallway.

The east exit was right there to her left. Straight ahead of her was the vending machine with the dead man keeping watch over the food. She was startled by several rats as they scurried over his bloating body and into the shadows. She covered her nose with her left hand at the smell. Then she looked to her left and saw the sidewalk illuminated by the full moon. Cautiously, she walked to the door and peered out into the night. Seeing no danger, she slipped out the door and walked stealthily to her right toward Pickitt Hall, all the while, hugging the east edge of the building.

Overwatch

Michael kept his vigilance as he peeked out through the branches of the maple tree above the crest of the roof. He was perched in an overwatch position on the north end of the west wing of the freshman dorm, Quincer Hall. The light of the moon illuminated everything around him, but he was concealed in the safety of the shadows of the big maple tree. A new moon would have been better since they all had night vision.

He could clearly see everything to his north, the big pond and then the Hansen Athletic Center. To the west he had a clear view of the back side of Pickitt Dormitory, the place where his father and the colonel were now entering. If she was alive, that's where they expected to find Bob's daughter as that was her dormitory. Bob was set up beneath a tree on the southwest corner of Pickitt, so they had all sides of the dorm covered. The plan was for Mag and the colonel to go into the dorm as a team and search the dorm one room at a time if need be. But first, they would go to Abbey's room and hope for the best. If she was dead, then they'd take her body home. If alive, well, that was the best-case scenario.

Michael also had a clear view to the east all the way to the admin building, but another tree obscured his line of sight to the south. His first choice had been the Welch clock tower, but he had no way of getting to the top, so he'd satisfied himself with this tree beside Quincer dorm.

Sounds carried a long way into the crisp, cold, night air, and Michael heard his father and the colonel enter Pickitt through the southeast entrance. It was unlikely they'd be able to surprise anyone with stealth, even with the help of night vision.

And then he looked to the north toward the Hansen Center and saw movement. He turned his rifle in that direction and moved the night vision scope up to his right eye.

Abby on the Move

THE LIGHT OF THE MOON WAS SO BRIGHT THAT SHE could see her shadow, and she didn't like that one bit. Over the past week she'd learned that darkness was her friend. She stuck to the south wall of the Hansen Center as she moved east down toward the pond, moving from tree to tree as best she could. Once she reached the bottom of the slope she'd be able to hug the edge of the pond near the tall grass and move from one tree to the next until she reached Pickitt. After that she'd have to sprint up to the back side as best she could without being seen.

She reached the pond and could hear the frogs singing as always. It was strange that she'd never noticed them before. There was a splash in the water to her right and it made her jump. Then she saw the white duck in the moonlight and calmed her heart-rate. *Calm down, Abby. This is your campus, your turf. There's no one here but you.*

And that's when the man spoke to her. "Hello, Abby."

Abby stifled a scream and her heart raced faster than it had the night she'd killed the man at the vending machine.

Pickitt Hall

Pickitt Hall had been built in 1970 and just a few weeks ago had been home to some 180 college girls. Its exterior was red and brown brick, like many of the buildings on campus, and it had three stories. The north end faced the large pond, and was also home to dozens of geese, ducks and swans that were notorious for spreading their waste all over the north lawn of the dorm.

Mag and Buzz were inside now, on the first floor. They started on the eastern end and were slowly working their way to the west, room by room. Just a few doors down they came to Abby's room. Using hand signals, the colonel instructed Mag to enter first. Mag entered and quickly fanned to the left. Buzz entered immediately behind him and fanned to the right.

They cleared the room quickly and found no one. Mag moved to the desk and saw a picture of Abby with some of her friends from the college. He picked it up, showed it to the colonel before shoving it inside his cargo pocket.

They silently moved to the next room. It took them 20 minutes to clear each room on the first floor.

"I've got movement on the south wall of the Hansen Sports Center. Looks like only one person."

Mag looked over at Buzz, who quickly acknowledged the call from Michael.

"Roger that. Do not engage unless fired upon, but keep us advised."

Mag and Buzz quickly moved up the stairwell to the next floor.

Philosophy by the Pond

ABBY MOVED HER JAVELIN TO THE THROWING POSItion and held it there.

"Are you really going to kill me, Abby?"

Abby recognized the voice, but couldn't quite place who it was. She pressed her back into the cat tails behind her.

"Who are you?"

She heard the man laugh softly. "Ah, a great philosophical question for the ages. You were always so astute and inquisitive. Always asking questions to which there are few satisfying answers."

The man was seated on a wooden bench beneath a small tree about 20 feet off the water's edge. Abby watched him in the shadow of the moon as he crossed his right leg over his left. He appeared to be wearing a suit and tie.

"Why are you here?"

The man laughed again, this time a bit louder and more sincere.

"Now there you go again, Miss Vandenberg, asking the most basic questions of the universe. *Who am I and why am I here?*" And then Abby put a name to the voice and lowered her javelin.

"I'll answer your questions seriatum." The man folded his arms across his chest to help ward off the cold and damp.

"First, Who am I. Why, the answer is simple and any freshman here knows that. I am a child of God." He paused, but Abby said nothing. "And second, Why am I here? That's also simple and basic. I exist to serve the will of my creator, and my father God." He motioned with his hand for Abby to come closer to the bench. "As I recall you got an A in my class, Miss Vandenberg. You should already know these things."

Abby stepped forward timidly. She was well aware that she hadn't taken a bath in close to 2 weeks, but, by the look and smell of things, neither had Professor McKnight.

"That's not what I meant, Dr. McKnight." The doctor was in his late fifties, with a head of sparsely scattered gray hair. He had a gray beard as well, neatly trimmed.

"What I mean is ... Well, I'm not sure what I mean."

He nodded. "Yes, I know. And I think you mean this: Why am I here at the college when half the world is dead, and it's obvious college will never again be in session? Is that what you mean to ask?"

Abby took a step closer and nodded. The professor responded. "Well, I suppose I could ask you the same question, Abby, but I won't. I assume you are here through a series of unfortunate events, whereas I'm here simply because my house is just a few blocks away." And then his eyes grew moist. "And, of course, there were more than a few unfortunate events in my own life."

Abby was standing in the shadows of the tree now in front of her old professor. "What happened? Did your wife die?" Dr. McKnight turned his head to the right and nodded slowly.

"Yes, that's exactly what happened. My two grown children and their family as well." The frogs continued singing in the background as though nothing bad or evil had ever happened in the world.

"I've always liked this bench, and I've been teaching here for 25 years. I raised my kids just a few blocks away." And then he hesitated. "Abby, I've been studying philosophy my entire adult life, and I've come to the conclusion that I still don't understand it."

Abby finally sat down on the far end of the bench. She kept the javelin in her hands between her legs with the butt end on the grass. The leaves had started to turn to yellow and red, and some had already fallen to the ground at her feet. She said nothing.

"It's like everything else, Abby. Some people study life while others all around them are too busy living life to study it."

The reflection of the moon was glistening on the waters of the pond now. "You know, Abby. Two weeks ago I would have thought this night was very beautiful, and I suppose it still is. But, I've been sitting here for the past 30 minutes trying to trick myself into thinking that everything is good and back to normal again. And I almost had myself fooled, but ... then I heard a gun shot and a scream from over to the west beyond the seminary, and I knew that someone had just died. It wasn't just one gun shot and one scream; it was a whole series of screams and shots."

He looked across the pond to the seminary building. "I imagine an entire family just died."

Abby spoke, softly at first, but then gradually got louder. "I killed a man day before yesterday. It was in the

Hansen Center by the vending machine. He's still there on the floor where I killed him." And then her eyes grew distant. "I had no preconceptions of killing a man. It's not something I ever thought about. It wasn't even on my radar. But ..." She looked out to the moon and then back down at the javelin. "When the time came, it happened so fast that I didn't think about it. I just stabbed him through the heart because I didn't want to die yet."

The philosophy professor turned away from the moon and looked into her face, just a few feet away. "That's very sad, Abby. I'm sorry that happened to you."

"And I'm sorry about your wife and family."

They both turned their eyes back out to the moonlit water. There was a clumsy silence for several seconds, but the frogs and the ducks filled in the gaps with background noise.

"So, what are you going to do, young lady?"

Abby grasped the javelin firmly in both hands. "Well, my parents live about 45 minutes south of here. I was thinking I'd go back to Pickitt Hall and rummage through the dead bodies until I find some car keys.

"I know it's stealing, but ... I don't know how much of a choice I have." She shrugged impotently. "I can't stay here forever, and it's too far to walk. There are so many dangers out there right now. But I want to get home to my mom and dad and my two brothers." She paused a moment. "Assuming they're still alive."

Dr. McKnight leaned back in the bench and unfolded his arms. He moved his lips a bit as if getting ready to say something important, then he sighed and let out with it.

"I don't think it's stealing anymore, Abby. Your friends are dead and with Jesus now. Sometimes us Christians get so heavenly minded that we're of no earthly good. I think you need to be a pragmatist right now." He sighed audibly. "So many Christians seem to think that God has no common sense." And then he turned to her and laughed. "I'm not implying that you have no common sense, Abby, it's just I think God looks as much at our hearts as he does our actions." And then he waited a moment as if by design. "God is very good with the 'why' questions. Us, not so much, but God ... God always knows why and he takes that into account."

Abby looked over at him, wishing she could see his face more clearly. "So you think God understands why I killed that man?"

Dr. McKnight nodded matter of factly. "Yes, dear. I think He does."

And then he laughed again. "And don't worry your pretty, little head about stealing a car." He waited for her to ask why, but she didn't. Then he pulled some jangling keys out of his suit pocket and took the silver key off the crowded ring. "It's the black Subaru parked up in the faculty lot the other side of the administration building." He handed her the key and she looked down at it and smiled.

"Go home to your family, Abby. They're waiting for you. I know they are."

Abby stood and stepped over to her professor. He stood and they embraced for just a moment.

"Thank you sir." And then she ran off toward the east.

The old man watched her go,and then sat back down on the bench to study the night. He still didn't feel good, but ... he did feel a whole lot less bad.

PHILOSOPHY IN THE APOCALYPSE

philosophy[fi-los-uh-fee]

noun, plural phi·los·o·phies.

the rational investigation of the truths and principles of being, knowledge, or conduct.

dictionary.com

The apocalypse can become very pragmatic very quickly, thus, altering your belief system. But here's the thing. The Christian belief system doesn't change no matter what the circumstances are. Why? Because it's all rooted in the personal relationship between God and man. No matter what happens here on earth, God never changes. He is immutable, unchanging, forever and ever, amen, and that's that.

Now, it can seem confusing as to how we apply that belief system during major changes in our life, but, in the end, it's all very simple.

During good times ... we praise Him.

During bad times ... we praise Him.

It's the details that seem to get us humans all wrapped around the axle. Don't sweat the small stuff. Praise God and serve Him and your fellow man and everything else is frosting on the cake.

Night Vision (NVIS)

When it comes to the end of the world as we know it, night vision will become a very rare and important commodity. In the military, we refer to it as a form of force multiplier. Just having it makes us more effective in combat.

NVIS can cost hundreds or it can cost thousands. Get the best you can afford, but it doesn't have to be the best or nothing. Generation 1 NVIS costs hundreds, but is still better than the human eye after dark.

In simple layman's terms:

Gen 1: Good out to 75 yards. Better than nothing. Has built-in illuminator, so you are visible to others with NVIS. Low resolution.

Price: $300 to $800

Gen 2: This is a big step up. Longer range, clearer and brighter images. Invisible to others with NVIS. Longer battery life and more reliable than gen 1. Price: $1,500 to $3,000

Gen 3: This is what Special Ops people use. Range is extended to over 300 yards. Clean, bright resolution. 10,000 hours of life expectancy.

Price: $3,000 to $6000

> *"The Lord is a warrior; the Lord is his name."*
>
> *Exodus 15:3 (NIV)*

CHAPTER 12

__Cornerstone University, Grand Rapids, MI__

MICHAEL SPOKE SOFTLY INTO the tiny voice-activated microphone. "I hear voices now over by the Hansen Center, down by the pond."

"Roger that. Just continue to monitor and report as necessary. We're finishing up with the third floor. We'll be heading out in about 5 minutes."

Michael strained to hear the voices. He couldn't be sure, but one sound like a man, and the other like a woman. He continued listening to the incoherent voices for the next five minutes, then heard the call from his father.

"We're coming out the southeast entrance now."

And that's when Michael heard the sound of the car engine off to the east of him. He looked over and saw the headlights turn on.

"Dad! There's a car just started up to my east!"

"Roger that. Do you have a visual?"

"Affirmative. I can see their head lights but not the car."

"Son, turn off the night vision on your scope and try again."

Michael followed his recommendation and soon had the small Subaru in his scope. "It looks black or dark blue. A small car, maybe foreign. It's heading to the East Beltline." He waited a few seconds. "It's headed south."

Mag answered his transmission. "Roger that. See if it gets on the highway or just continues south on the Beltline."

Michael waited, but lost a visual on the car. There were just too many obstacles in the way. "I lost them Dad."

"Turn your night vision back on and check again. Just follow the light."

Michael again did as he was told and was amazed at how bright the light became. "Looks like they continued on south down the Beltline."

There was a minute or so of silence before the reply came. "Roger that. Come on down and rendezvous at the rally point ASAP."

"Roger that."

Michael carefully slung his carbine across his back and slowly climbed down the tree by the light of the moon so as not to damage his equipment. Once on the ground he ran over to the front of the Corum building where the other three were already waiting.

Bob Vandenberg looked exhausted and extremely dejected. Everyone looked to the colonel for instructions. He glanced over at Bob, then down at his wristwatch. "We still have time. Let's check the other girl's dormitories the same way we checked this one." And then he turned to

Michael and Bob. "We can double our speed if the two of you also clear rooms as a team. You two take Keithley Hall and Mag and I will go for Cook. Got it?"

The two teams divided up and soon were clearing rooms in their respective buildings. Michael and Bob completed their building first and Michael called it in.

"Nothing in Keithley."

The reply was instant. "Move to the cafeteria. Check it out but be alert."

They both moved to the building but had to break glass to get in. The noise sounded tremendous. Fifteen minutes later they emerged with nothing to show for their time.

They met the colonel and Mag at the Christ Chapel and all did a room-by-room search there. They found a few dead bodies in the pews, but no living creature. Next, they went to Faber Hall. Michael and Bob took the ground floor while the other team took the stairs to the second floor.

Michael and Bob found nothing, that's when they heard gunshots from upstairs.

"Dad, are you okay?"

Nothing. Then two more gunshots. And these weren't from AR-15s.

"Dad! Come in. Are you okay?"

There was no answer, so Michael ran to the stairway. He heard someone coming down and raised his carbine with his finger on the trigger. He looked into the night scope and saw a man carrying a pistol. He confirmed it wasn't his father or Buzz before pressing the trigger multiple times. The man stumbled and then came crashing down the rest of the stairs.

"Dad, come in. Sit rep!"

There was no reply.

"Dad, I'm coming upstairs. Don't shoot me."

Michael bounded up the rest of the stairs and burst through the doorway. To his left was an open area beside the elevators. He saw two bodies on the ground and rushed over. He turned them over and saw three rounds in the first chest and four in the other. Neither man was Buzz or his father. One man had an AR-15 on a sling, and the other had a double-barrelled shotgun and a pistol.

Then he heard voices down the hallway and headed south just as Bob was coming up the stairs.

"Hold this in place, Mag. Push down hard."

Michael saw empty brass now on the floor and then light from a flashlight. He recognized the colonel's voice.

"Don't shoot, colonel, I'm coming in."

"Advance! Hurry!"

Michael ran up to the office complex on the left and burst through the door. There on the floor sat Buzz and his father in a pool of blood. It was already soaking into the carpet tiles.

"What happened?"

Buzz wasted no words with his answer. "I don't know if it went through or not. Lots of blood. May have missed the artery, but we've got to plug it up."

Buzz pulled open an envelope and quickly tore it open.

"What is that stuff?"

"It's combat gauze, just compressed gauze bandage filled with Quik-Clot. Aids in blood clotting." He rammed it down into the wound and pressed hard. Then he pressed a large pressure bandage onto the wound as well and then secured it all as best he could with a lot of tape.

"Press down on this and hold it while I go get the truck."

Just then Bob staggered in. He wasn't in the same

shape as Michael, and his adrenaline dump had just about exhausted him.

"Follow me. Now!"

Bob complied despite his aching muscles. They headed for the stairs but were met with gunfire at the bottom.

"Stop moving, Bob. We have night vision, let's use it!"

Buzz donned his night vision goggles and began to search out the direction of the shots. Bob stayed behind him. After several seconds, the colonel located the sniper and dispatched him with one shot to the head.

More shots rang out as other unknowns returned fire. Buzz took cover behind a steel window frame as best he could. He felt the impact of hand gun rounds hitting the front of his vest.

"That's it! These guys wanna dance, let's oblige 'em!"

Bob just shook his head in confusion. "I'm a farmer. I don't know what that means."

Buzz tore off his night vision and reached into a camo sachel on his waist and pulled out three fragmentation grenades. "Watch and learn, farm boy!"

He pulled the pins and threw each grenade one at a time. Just as the last grenade cleared the stairwell, the first one exploded.

The blast shook the whole building, throwing down ceiling tiles and plaster and wood and masonry everywhere. When the smoke and dust cleared, Buzz put his night vision goggles back on and scanned for survivors.

He saw movement and aimed and fired. The movement stopped. "Okay, farm boy, we rush them on my count."

He turned to Bob for confirmation, but all he got was a blank look. Bob yelled at him as loud as he could.

"I can't hear you! I can't hear a thing!"

Buzz shook his head in disgust."Amateurs!"

Then he burst out of the stairwell like a 20-year-old boy and headed past the security desk up front. There was no one there, so he cleared the lobby and then the book store. He saw a man crawling away from the fight, so he walked up behind him and put one shot to the back of his head.

Then he heard Michael over the comms. "Colonel, what's going on? Do you need back-up?"

Buzz smiled. He was starting to like this boy. "Negative, soldier. Stay with the wounded. I'm gettin' the evac wheels. How's our boy doing?"

"He's awake now, and the bleeding seems to be slow-ing."

Buzz smiled. They just might make it out of here alive after all. "Keep the pressure on and your eyes open. There could be more of them upstairs. We didn't have time to clear it. But the downstairs is clear for now. I'll send farm boy up to help. Try not to shoot him."

He turned and yelled over to Bob, but he still couldn't hear him. He walked over to him and yelled directly into his ear. "Go upstairs and do a room-clearing. Watch Michel's back! I'm getting the truck."

Bob nodded and headed off up the stairs. The colonel headed for the door and the southern parking lot.

"You okay, Dad?" Michael looked down at his dad, all the while pressing tight against the clotting shoul-der.

Mag answered in labored breaths. "Yeah, I think so. I think it missed the bone. What's the situation?"

"Buzz is getting the truck, Should be about 5 minutes."

Mag looked over into the darkness past the media room. "There could be more of them up here. Let's get downstairs and be ready when the colonel pulls up."

Just then Bob bounded up the stairs and gunfire erupted once more. Bob went down hard in the lounge area in front of the elevators and didn't move. Michael looked at his dad for instructions. Mag pointed to his night vision scope and then to the media communications department. Michael nodded his understanding and moved slowly and quietly toward the hallway door. He peeked out and used his night vision to search for targets. He saw none. Then he heard a sound from the southern end of the hallway. He rotated his head slowly and then he saw them. Two men crouching down and moving slowly toward him.

Michael raised his AR-15 and shot center mass. The first man went down and groaned on the floor. The second man hopped to his right into a room. The door was partially open, but Michael didn't want to go in after him. It seemed like suicide. He thought for a moment and then pulled a frag grenade out of his sachel, removed the safety clip and pulled the pin. The door was open 45 degrees out into the hallway, so he threw the grenade. It banked off the angled door, and caromed inside the room. Michael plugged his ears.

After the explosion, he rushed down the hallway and peeked into the room, careful to use the cement block wall as cover. The room was empty, and there was a door leading from the back into the office complex where he'd left his father. That's when he heard gun fire, and then a loud thud as someone fell to the floor.

Michael ran back and saw a dead man lying on top of his father who was trying desperately to get the man off him. Michael knelt down and pulled the man away and let him drop to the floor beside his father.

Just then Michael and Mag heard their comms roar to

life. "I'll be there in 2 minutes. Be out there and ready to roll!"

Michael responded. "Roger that."

"Wait here, Dad. I have to check on Bob."

Mag laughed, then coughed. "Right. Like I'm going any where."

Bob was lifting himself off the floor just as Michael walked up to him. "You okay?"

Bob nodded. I think so. Just got the wind knocked outta me when I hit the ground. Michael saw blood flowing from the man's head, but decided to deal with that later.

"Help me with Dad. Buzz is almost here."

Michael helped his father get to his feet, and then shouldered him to the door. "Bob, get all these rifles and magazines, as many as you can carry. We'll take them with us."

It never occurred to Bob that he was obeying the combat commands of a 16-year-old boy, just that what he was saying made good sense, and that Michael was in charge of his emotions. So he complied as Michael helped his father down the stairwell.

"Cover us from the rear!"

Bob picked up an AR-15 that was beside a dead body, then stripped off three full magazines. Then he followed them down the stairs.

Michael held his AR up and hanging from his one-point sling as he tread down the stairs. By time they reached the lobby, they could hear the roar of Mag's truck.

"We're coming out, colonel. Don't shoot."

"Roger that You're clear to evac!"

Buzz met them at the door with his AR up and ready, but there were no more targets inside or out.

"Lay him down in the back of the cab seat. Michael I

want you in shotgun position."

They both complied and soon Buzz was driving away from the campus at a high rate of speed. They pulled back onto the highway and headed east to Cascade again. Once at the 36th street exit, they pulled off and coasted to a stop on the shoulder of the road.

"Michael, take overwatch! I have to check on your father."

Michael put on his father's night vision goggles and jumped out onto the hood of the truck with his carbine. He searched all four directions, but saw no one.

"Mag, tell me what's going on inside you."

Mag turned his head to look at the colonel. He smiled as best he could. "I feel weak."

Buzz took his pulse. It was steady but weak. He opened his left eye and shined a light into it then took it away.

"Bob, when I get out of here I want you to prop that pack under his ankles so he gets more blood to his head. Then sit on the floor and keep him from rolling off the seat. Got it?"

Bob's hearing was coming back now, so he nodded, and Buzz hurried back into the driver's seat. "Get back in here, Michael!"

Ten seconds later they were headed right onto 36th street. Buzz got the truck up past 100 miles per hour. They had to slow down again to turn left onto Patterson, but then Buzz opened it up and they hardly saw the airport as it whizzed by on the left. They slowed down to cross the Beltline and made the turn south.

Buzz turned his head to the west and looked toward Patterson ... and that's when everything went wrong.

My First Grenade

Most of my readers have never touched a fragmentation grenade, so the only picture they have of a grenade comes through Hollywood movies. As is often the case, Hollywood isn't always real life. I remember being surprised back in 1976 when I threw my first and only hand grenade. It was the M67 Grenade, and it wasn't shaped correctly. In the John Wayne movies I'd always watched as a kid, they had a pineapple shape. (The pineapple grenade was used extensively in World War II and had the official designation of Mk 2 Grenade.) But the one the drill instructor placed in my hand was round, and it was about the size of a baseball. I still remember his exact words "Remove safety clip. Pull pin, twist and pull."

It was easy. I pulled the pin and threw it as far as I could before dropping down behind the cement wall. Then it blew up and hurt my ears a bit. I remember being scared, but it was an exciting fear.

The M67 Grenade has a fuse delay of 4 to 5.5 seconds. It weights 14 ounces, is 2.5 inches in diameter and is 3.53 inches tall. The 6.5 ounces of explosive inside is called Composition B, which is a mixture of RDX and TNT.

The M67 was designed in the late 1950s and was in common use in the US military from 1968 to the present. The M67 has an injury radius of 49 feet and a fatality radius of 16 feet.

BEHIND THE SCENES LOOK

I attended Cornerstone University from 1977 to 1982, receiving my bachelor's degree in English. That's where I wrote my very first novel, which has since been lost and, thankfully, will never see the light of day. Back then Cornerstone was called Grand Rapids Baptist College and was about half the size it is now. Many of the buildings I wrote about in this chapter weren't yet built, but I'm still familiar with the campus because my daughter also attended the college and graduated from there in 2018.

I was also honored to teach at Cornerstone as an Adjunct Professor for three years. I taught a writing class to journalism students called *Scientific and Technical Writing*.

I taught the class in Faber Hall, which is where the gun and grenade battle occurred in the last chapter. Because I taught in that building every week, I was able to picture it in my head as I wrote, lending rich details to the story. The room where I held my class is exactly where the final hostile was killed.

> *"Dear friend, do not imitate what is evil but what is good. Anyone who does what is good is from God. Anyone who does what is evil has not seen God."*
>
> *3 John 1:1 (NIV)*

CHAPTER 13

The Big Chase

WHEN ABBY LEFT THE COL-
lege, she drove straight down East
Beltline. She passed Michigan Avenue
and then Fulton and Cascade without seeing another vehicle. In fact, she didn't see a single light in any of the
houses or businesses that she drove by.

As she approached Burton Street, Abby looked to
the right and saw Calvin College. She was familiar with
Calvin, because sometimes Cornerstone and Calvin
played each other in athletic activities. She slowed just
past the overhead pedestrian bridge that spanned East
Beltline. There, on the side of the road was a County
Sheriff cruiser. It was parked diagonally and a dead dep-
uty was sprawled on the shoulder about ten feet from the
car. About 20 yards past the policeman was a smaller
campus security vehicle. It was turned over on its side,

and Abby could tell that it had been set on fire. Her first instinct was to slow down and pull over, but she thought again and didn't do that. Instead, Abby turned the wheel to the left, giving the two ghostly shells a wide berth.

She accelerated through the Burton intersection. Obedience was so ingrained in her psyche, that she found it difficult to disobey traffic laws, even though it was obvious that traffic laws were now obsolete and perhaps even a detriment to her own safety.

She approached 28th street with extreme caution. She rolled her window down a few inches, so she could hear what was going on outside. A few gun shots rang out over by Woodland Mall, and she flinched in her car seat. Part of her wanted to ram her foot down on the gas pedal and get out of there as fast as possible, but the other side of her, the side that had been conditioned by society to blindly follow the rules, held her back.

Abby saw lights in the huge parking lot of Woodland Mall. There were about five cars there with men outside the vehicles yelling at each other. She heard more gunshots, then, finally, her self-preservation instinct kicked in and she pushed down hard on the accelerator. The little Subaru lurched reluctantly forward. As she crossed 28th street, two cars pulled away from the curb and started to follow her.

Abby didn't know what to do. She'd been raised on a farm, then gone to a Christian school where everyone was nice and calm and gentle, all practicing the golden rule and showing kindness and compassion for one another. It was then that Abby came to the stark realization that she was neither mentally nor emotionally prepared for city life without the rule of law. She needed to get back to the farm. She pressed the accelerator down as far as it would go, not stopping until she felt the floorboard. The little Subaru, hesitated, as if complaining, but gradually picked up speed.

The two cars were late model cars: a Ford Mustang and a Camaro. Within a half mile they had closed the gap to nothing and were directly behind, just a few feet off her bumper. Abby was terrified, but kept driving straight ahead. She passed 32nd Street where the Beltline turned into a divided road. The Camaro behind her sped up quickly and pulled into the left lane. It was soon beside her.

Two young men were hanging out the passenger side windows clear up to their waists. They were yelling and laughing as loud as they could, encouraging her to pull over so they could show her a good time. Finally, the fear inside her began to dissipate, and was slowly replaced with anger and determination.

The transition was surprising to her, almost scary in a way. She'd never felt like this before, nor had she ever acted in total disregard for her own safety or the safety of others while driving a car. Without thinking, she turned the steering wheel quickly to the left and rammed into the brand new Camaro. One man immediately lost his grip and fell out onto the pavement. The Mustang behind them swerved violently to try and miss him, but ended up plowing headlong into the concrete barrier of the median wall. The Mustang flipped end over end and crashed onto the pavement.

She was passing 44th street now, and the second man was now separated from the Camaro and hanging on to her Subaru with his right hand on the open window and the other attached to the side, rear-view mirror. Abby reached down and pressed the electric window switch and the glass tightened on the man's hand, making him scream all the more. His feet were dragging on the pavement as he yelled for her to stop. That gave her an idea.

Abby let up on the gas and slammed on the brake pedal. The man shot off the side of her car so fast she didn't see it happening. Once he was gone she pressed on the gas pedal again. She looked down onto her lap and screamed as loud as she could. The man's fingers were laying on her lap, bloody and torn.

The Camaro was now a hundred yards ahead of her and slowing down in the left-hand lane. They passed the 52nd street intersection. The Camaro was beside her now, and the man in the driver's seat aimed a pistol at her and started shooting. One shot ricocheted off the rear-view mirror inside the car and went out the passenger-side window, breaking the glass. The next shot hit her in the front of her forehead, leaving a long and bloody crease, but only skin-deep. The blood ran down into her eyes, obscuring her vision, so she took her left hand off the wheel and wiped away as much of the blood as she could until she could see again.

She stepped on the brakes again, and the little Subaru dropped back and the shooting stopped. But the Camaro also slowed and the driver was soon shooting at her again. That's when Abby looked in the rear-view mirror and saw the flashing red and blue lights from the state police cruiser behind her. She immediately thanked God for her rescue and began to slow down some more.

The police car whizzed by her and rammed the Camaro from behind, causing it to slam into the concrete divider, lose complete control and then run off the road to the right. The Camaro hit a power pole and knocked it over, coming to a complete stop. Steam started to rise up from under the hood.

Abby craned her neck as she drove by the wrecked car, but the police cruiser slowed and came to an abrupt stop directly beside it. A few seconds later, Abby heard over a dozen gunshots. They faded as she drove away, leaving the carnage and death behind her.

Abby pressed the accelerator again, and was relieved to see the Patterson street turn coming up on her right. She turned on her turn signal out of habit and was soon driving south east toward home. With any luck, in another 30 minutes she'd be safe and sound in her driveway back in Hickory Flats.

But those hopes were suddenly dashed, when she looked in her rear-view mirror again and saw the same police cruiser turn onto Patterson Road and accelerate quickly, all the while, lights flashing and siren blaring.

ABBY DIDN'T FEEL RIGHT ABOUT PULLING OVER FOR the police officer, but ... she didn't feel right about disobeying him either. She tried to think it through, but there just wasn't time, and she had to make a decision. She reasoned that she had no choice but to comply, so she turned on her right blinker and slowed to a stop on the shoulder of the road. She turned on her emergency blinkers and her dome light as well, exactly the way she'd been taught. She was careful to leave her seat belt on just so she wouldn't get a ticket. Then she rolled her window halfway down and pulled her drivers license out of the back pocket of her jeans. Two weeks ago all those things would have been the right thing to do, but now ... she just wasn't sure. And then she looked over in the passenger seat and saw the bloody javelin propped up against it.

She glanced at her rear-view mirror, but is was gone,

probably ripped off by the man who'd been holding on to her car. The police siren turned off. Quickly, she grabbed the javelin and threw it onto the floor in the back seat. Just then, there was a knock on her window. She looked up and saw the man standing there, but he didn't look like a police officer. He was wearing blue jeans and a hoodie, and he carried a Glock pistol in his right hand. He lifted the hoodie and she saw him smile. It made her blood run cold. She quickly hit the door lock button.

Just then the second man wrapped his knuckles on the passenger-side window.

"Please step out of the vehicle, ma'am."

Abby was so afraid that she could hardly talk, but she forced herself to regain her composure and to think clearly.

"Uh, sir. Thank you for saving me."

The man didn't stop smiling. "Just open up this door and you can thank me personally."

Abby wiped the blood off her brow and then turned to see the other man standing there by the passenger door. He seemed to be looking around as if nervous.

"C'mon, Tarish. Get 'er outta the car, so we kin get outta here! I don't like sittin' the side a the road, specially after what just happened. More guys'll be here, and I don't wanna share with 'em. This girl looks mighty fine, even with all the blood."

The man in the hoodie wrapped the glass again, this time with the muzzle of his Glock. "C'mon, girl. You know this is happenin' so's you might as well hop on outta the car so we can get it done. Ain't nobody gonna save ya. The cops er all dead."

The man on the other side egged her on as well. "Yeah, girl, ya come out now and we'll be romantic 'n gentle like, but if ya make us break in there ... it won't be so much fun fer you."

Abby wasn't thinking clearly. "You're not police officers are you?"

Both men laughed hysterically. They were in their late teens or early twenties. "No kiddin' lady! So if ya don't haul yer pretty butt outta the car, then we'll put you with the cops."

The other man added. "Yeah, we got both of 'em dead in the trunk."

Abby whispered a prayer. *God please help me!* And then the man at the passenger window smashed the glass with his gun and it shattered inward. He reached into the car and grabbed her arm, but Abby fought back. She desperately flung herself into the back seat and grabbed onto the javelin.

The other man reached in and unlocked the door. Abby stabbed his hand with the javelin and he drew back with a string of profanities. Blood spurted out his right hand and he dropped the Glock onto the front seat as he stepped away from the car.

Abby lunged for the gun just as the man from the passenger side launched himself into the car. She missed the grip of the pistol, and the man was on her back now, wrapping his arms around her in a bear hug. This seemed familiar to her, like the man she'd killed at the vending machine. Instinctively, she threw her head back as hard as she could, cracking her skull into the man's nose over and over again. She felt his grip loosen and she tried to turn around, but the man was already regaining his strength.

He took his Glock and started to beat her on the head over and over again. That's when the second man reached into the car through the window and grabbed her around the throat. Abby felt his hands tighten around her carotid artery and windpipe. Savagely, the second man began to squeeze harder and harder.

The first man stopped hitting her and started to laugh maniacally. He threw his Glock down onto the floor so he could use both hands.

"Hold her down, man. Don't let 'er squirm so much. I got stuff to do."

The other man seemed angry. "I get first this time! You went first yesterday!"

"Just shut up 'n hold er down! You go when I say you go!"

The first man grabbed onto her shirt and ripped down as hard as he could. Abby felt the fabric tear and give way. The cold, night air rushed against her bare skin, and she knew what was about to happen. She couldn't let it, but ... they were both so strong.

The man pressed his mouth against her lips, and she bit him as hard as she could. He screamed in pain while the other man, with his hands still around her throat started to laugh.

"On second thought, you kin go first."

The angry man punched her in the head over and over again. Abby tried to block his blows but he pushed her feeble attempts away like a giant swatting a fly.

Finally, with all her strength ebbing out of her limbs, Abby gave up and lowered her hands to the seat. The man smiled.

"There ya go. That's a good girl."

Abby's right hand fell against the Glock and she grasped it like a lifeline, raised it up and fired three times into the man's chest. He fell back away with a look of fear and shock on his face before falling out the door and onto the shoulder of the road. It reminded Abby of the other man she'd killed, and the man who'd been holding on to the side of her car right before his fingers had been ripped off and he'd been brutally thrown to the pavement.

She felt the second man's fingers loosen around her throat. She turned as quickly as she could and raised the gun again. The man's eyes got really big as the first flash lit up the night and the loud boom echoed inside the car. The round hit him in the belly and he sank down onto the pavement and tried to crawl back to the police cruiser.

Abby didn't want him to get away. It wasn't hatred or revenge, she just wanted to make sure he couldn't come back or send his friends back to hurt her. She opened the car door and fell out onto the pavement. Abby aimed at the crawling man who now pressed his hands against his bleeding gut.

"Don't lady! I wasn't gonna do nothin'!"

But Abby didn't believe him. She pressed the trigger again and again and again. The gun jumped wildly in her hands. Most of the rounds didn't hit. But some did. The man slumped his head to the road and it hit with a crack.

Abby felt dizzy and sick to her stomach. She dropped the Glock and laid her head down as softly as she could. The pain was there and growing. She whispered out loud. "Thank you God." Her head hurt so bad. And then she went to sleep on the side of the road.

Once again, the world became quiet. The bright lights of the police cruiser continued to light up the night as crickets and frogs sang innocently from a wet, marshy puddle in the field beside the road.

GLOCK TRIVIA

- Gaston Glock developed the first working prototype for the Glock 17 pistol in 1982. It took him 3 months. Prior to that, he had zero experience in firearms design.

- The Glock 17 was so named because it was the 17th patent procured by the company.

- The Glock 17, though hugely popular now, was not readily received in the United States. The very idea of a "plastic" gun was rejected by many in law enforcement. They thought it would break too easily.

- Gun control activists inadvertently helped boost interest and sales for the original Glock pistol. They claimed it was made mostly of plastic and would not register on a metal detector, thus making it dangerous and likely to be used by criminals. They were mistaken.

WHY THE GLOCK FOR PREPPING?

- As a general rule, Glocks are known for their toughness. I have several myself, and I can attest to this. I'm very rough on my guns. I shoot a lot of rounds, I get them wet, and I don't enjoy cleaning guns. Glocks are like the Timex of the gun world: they take a licking and they keep on ticking!

- Many Glocks are chambered in 9mm NATO. That means that ammo will be easier to come by in the event of shortages here in the United States. It also means great selection and cheap ammo prices.

- Glocks have a simple design with fewer moving parts than other semi-automatic pistols. That means fewer parts to break.

- Glock pistols are everywhere. It is undeniably one of the most popular handguns on the planet. As such, spare parts during an apocalypse will be easier to find. It also means there's a huge selection of after-market parts and accessories.

- Glock parts are interchangeable. Many of their models can swap out parts such as the Glock 17 and the Glock 19. This is handy in the apocalypse.

> *"So he took his men, divided them into three companies and set an ambush in the fields. When he saw the people coming out of the city, he rose to attack them."*
>
> *Judges 9:43 (NIV)*

CHAPTER 14

**On the Way Home**

"**W**HAT DO WE DO NOW, colonel?" Michael was staring up ahead at the red and blue strobes flashing on the side of Patterson Road. The colonel slowed down a bit. They were already running dark, using the night vision goggles, but the strobes were messing it up for the colonel. He took them off his head and took another look. He quickly pulled over to the shoulder of the road.

"This doesn't make any sense, boys. Why is a State Trooper making a traffic stop during the end of days?"

Buzz left the truck in drive and kept the engine running. He took the pair of binoculars off the console and raised them to his eyes.

"Those aren't cops up there. We've got three dead people on the pavement, and not a uniform in the bunch."

He handed the optics over to Michael, who quickly raised them up to his eyes. "Two men and a woman. I wonder what that was all about?"

Buzz reached down to the drop holster on his right leg and drew his Glock Model 17. He dropped the magazine to confirm it was fully loaded, then popped it back in the magazine well before doing a chamber check and quickly reholstering.

"I don't know, but I bet it had something to do with that Mustang and the Camaro back there. I saw two dead bodies on the street not counting the driver inside the Camaro and the ones inside the Mustang. Those boys had a major shoot-out back there."

Michael was still looking through the binoculars. Buzz called to Bob in the back seat. "What's Mag looking like that back there?"

"He's asleep now. His color looks better though and the bleeding is stopped. Pulse is steady but elevated. I'm no doctor, but I don't think we should dilly-dally around here though unless we want him to die in his sleep."

The colonel nodded his head. "Yeah. Good point." And then he looked in the rear-view mirror to see if anyone was approaching from behind them. "Did you see all those cars back there in the mall parking lot? They could pop up on us at any minute. I say we blow this pop stand while we still can."

Michael was starting to get an uneasy feeling in the pit of his stomach. He looked at the bumper of the black car. There were two stickers there, both of them advertising the radio station WCSG. He moved the binoculars over to look at the woman on the ground. There was a puddle of blood by her head on the pavement. He brought the optics back down to rest on his lap.

"Colonel. I think we should stop and check this out."

Buzz looked at Michael like he was crazy. "Son, your dad is bleeding in the back seat here. He needs to get home and the sooner the better. We can't afford to get into another fire fight."

He lifted his right foot off the brake and started to coast forward. But Michael raised his voice.

"No! We need to stop and check this out! There's something wrong here."

Buzz put his foot back on the brake. "Listen son. We're not stopping. Your dad needs medical attention, and I'm already out of adrenaline for one night. We're going back to base!"

And then Michael stopped him in his tracks. "I think that's the car that left the parking lot back at Cornerstone University."

Buzz looked over at him and frowned. "And why do you say that?"

Michael looked out the window to his right and then quickly back over to the colonel. "It's a black Subaru and it has a WCSG radio sticker on both sides of the back bumper. How many of those could there be?"

The colonel thought about it. Then he looked back over at the boy skeptically. "Are you sure, soldier?"

Michael pursed his lips tighter together. He wanted to say that he was, but ... there was a doubt.

"Not 100 percent, but pretty close. And, I keep think-ing ... is it possible that Abby is driving that car?" He glanced into the back seat but avoided eye contact with Bob Vandenberg. "I think we owe it to her to at least stop and check."

The tall farmer rotated on the floor and looked out the windshield. He craned his neck to see better, but he was still down too low.

"Let me get out and stand on top of the truck bed to get a better look at her. I ought to be able to recognize my own daughter."

The colonel contemplated the request for just a moment. They were a sitting duck here on the roadside. Finally, he nodded his approval and Bob opened the back door of the cab and slid himself out. He took the binoculars from Michael and jumped up into the truck bed.

"Michael, you go back there with him. You're overwatch. You see anything hostile and you shoot it. No questions asked."

Michael nodded and quickly jumped out of the cab and into the back of the truck to the right of Bob. He raised his carbine and looked through the night vision into the grass at the right shoulder of the road, looking for any hidden danger. Then he swung the scope left and repeated the process on the other side of the road.

"I see nothing bad up there, colonel. Just three dead people bleeding out on the pavement. No one else in the cars that I can tell."

But Buzz still didn't like it. All they had to do was get up to speed and push straight through and keep heading home, or better yet, keep driving down the Beltline and go around the police cruiser altogether. But Bob Vandenberg's voice stopped them all cold.

"That might be my daughter!"

The colonel shifted up in his seat. "Are you sure?"

There was a pause. "Well, no. Not entirely sure, but it looks like it might be her."

Buzz swore under his breath. And that was the clincher. No matter whether it was her or not; there was a chance it was her, so they'd have to check it out even if it was an ambush. If they didn't then Bob would always wonder if he'd left his little girl dead on the side of the road.

The colonel thought about it. He was already coming up with a plan.

ABBY'S HEAD WAS THROBBING LIKE A BASS DRUM AT a rock concert, and every time she tried to lift it up, it protested with a penalty of pain. She had no idea how long she'd been unconscious. It was still dark out, and the police cruiser was still there. She could even see the flashing lights with her eyes completely closed.

Her body ached in every conceivable place. There must be broken bones for it to hurt this much. She thought about her parents, her brothers, her church. She'd always assumed that after graduation she'd become a doctor, marry a handsome man who thought the sun rose and set on her; then she'd have three kids: two girls and a boy. They'd grow up healthy and smart and excel at everything they did. One would be a state soccer champ. The other would win the Nobel Prize for advances in physics. And the third would be a famous author and win the Pulitzer prize for literature. *Was that really too much to ask?* She didn't think so.

And then she and her husband would live to a ripe, old age, sitting in their rocking chairs on their porch as they watched the sun set and listened to the spring peepers after a long, hard, Michigan winter. Well, apparently that was too much to ask, because she'd been beaten, tossed on the road and left to die, and she still had no idea if her family was dead or alive.

But she pushed all the negativity out of her mind and tried to focus on the task at hand. After five minutes of lying there, she tried again to move. Abby managed to rotate her body around 180 degrees so that her head was pointed back to the door of the car. The car door was still open, so she lifted her hand up and grabbed onto the seat. She pulled and started to lift herself, but as soon as she lifted her head, the dizziness returned and she collapsed back down onto the pavement.

Perhaps she'd just rest here a little while longer.

As THE TRUCK INCHED ITS WAY FORWARD, MICHAEL and Bob kept a watchful eye. Michael stayed atop the truck bed where he had a birds eye view, while Bob walked along the right shoulder of the road using the engine block for cover.

About 40 yards further ahead, Buzz turned the wheel to the right and drove onto Patterson Road. He was coasting along at only 2 miles per hour, but it didn't take long before they were a mere 100 yards away from the police cruiser and the dead bodies. They had a simple plan; they'd just creep forward, using the truck for cover as they moved up onto the ambush site. All three men had their comms turned on.

"Overwatch?"

"Nothing from up here?"

"Right flank?"

Bob also acknowledged in the negative.

They kept inching forward.

"Colonel. I see movement!"

Buzz stepped on the brake.

"Report!"

There was a moment of silence.

"It's the woman. I think she's moving. She's alive!"

Bob Vandenberg couldn't maintain radio silence any longer. "Is it Abby? Can you see?"

There was a pause. "Negative, Bob. She's facing away from me."

The colonel broke into their conversation. "Maintain radio discipline. Don't watch the girl. Watch the men and the high grass to the left and right. You see movement - you shoot it."

Buzz took his foot off the brake again and coasted forward, all the while, looking to the left shoulder up ahead and sometimes in the rear-view mirror.

"Anything to our rear, Michael?"

"Negative. We're clear behind."

They were 25 yards behind the state police cruiser now, and Buzz braked again. He put the truck in park but left the engine running. He opened the drivers-side door and got out slowly and alertly. He held his carbine in front attached to his sling.

"Overwatch. Stay alert."

"Farm boy. Go right into the grass and secure the area. I'll turn off the cruiser lights and then I'll go left."

Buzz moved forward to the open cruiser door, reached in and turned off the engine. Then he turned off the headlights and strobes. Both men quickly pulled down their night vision goggles and everything lit up like day time. They had the advantage. Both men fanned out and into the grass at the sides of the road. They quickly cleared the roadside with the aid of their night vision.

Then Bob checked out the girl from closer up while Mag secured the forward flank.

And then they heard a scream.

GANG ACTIVITY IN THE APOCALYPSE

According to the latest stats, the number of criminal gangs in the United States is well over 30.000. The number of actual gang members in the United States is almost 1,000,000 people. Gang members are composed primarily of young men in their prime. Over half of them live in large cities, with another 25 percent operating in the suburbs and 15 percent in smaller cities. Only 5 percent reside in rural counties.

Gang activity accounts for a large portion of the drug crimes and violence that goes on in America. To a large degree, gang violence is kept to a minimum by the constant work of communities and law enforcement. But here's the big question: What happens when law enforcement is no longer there as a deterrent?

This last chapter showed us the answer. When law enforcement is no longer there to hold the wolves at bay, then it's Katy bar the door, because anyone with a predisposition for violence will take advantage of society's weakest members.

COVER VS CONCEALMENT

So many of us get our concept of a gun fight by watching Hollywood movies. But Hollywood is not real life. In this last chapter, the colonel made good use of the engine block on his truck to stop potential gun fire. In the movies, car doors will stop hundreds of bullets. But in real-life, car doors are nothing more than two layers of thin metal, separated by air.

Always remember that cover will stop a bullet, whereas concealment will only hide you. In an urban environment or in your home, there is very little true cover. Cover is made of thick metal, masonry or several inches of solid wood.

When you hide behind cover, remember to expose as little of yourself as possible. The basic rule is this: "Only show what you want to get shot." But you have to show at least your eyes, on occasion, or you won't be able to return fire.

And here's another important fact. During a gun fight, people have a tendency to shoot at only what they can visually see. I once saw a real-life gunfight where a man took cover behind a candy bar rack. His attacker failed to shoot through the rack, choosing instead to wait for him to step out. The other man shot through the rack, killing the attacker.

Bottom line: know what is true cover and use it whenever possible.

> *"Her officials within her are like wolves tearing their prey; they shed blood and kill people to make unjust gain."*
>
> *Ezekiel 22:27 (NIV)*

CHAPTER 15

Saving the Girl

MICHAEL TENSED WHEN HE heard Bob scream. He'd been scanning the right shoulder of the road for movement, but he quickly brought his AR-15 back to the center of the road where Bob was standing over the woman's body.

"It's Abby! Somebody help me get her up!"

Michael jumped down off the truck and onto the pavement before racing over to his friend. Bob was on his knees now, rolling her onto her back. He cradled her head in his hands and began to scream again, this time weeping uncontrollably.

"Michael, she's dead. My little girl is dead!" Michael knelt down beside him on the pavement and moved his hand to her throat to check for a pulse. Just then Buzz ran over from the left side of the road.

"No. She's alive. She has a pulse."

Michael could hardly believe how much her face was swollen and bruised. He hardly recognized her. He noticed the torn shirt and quickly moved the garment to better cover her up.

Just then Buzz came up behind them and took control. "Bob, get your daughter in the truck. Stay in the back with her and make her as comfortable as possible. We need to get home as quick as we can."

He turned to Michael. "Michael, check the car for anything we need to take with us. Make sure the two men are really dead. Then get back in the truck so we can move out."

Michael moved quickly. He checked the first man, saw the bullet holes in his belly, chest and face and moved on to the next man to the right of the car. He'd fallen out onto the ground with three rounds to the chest. He quickly reached down and checked his throat for a pulse. Finding nothing, he looked into the car. He grabbed Abby's pack and then noticed the javelin. He picked it up and brought it back to the truck bed.

"Michael, don't forget to gather up their weapons. We don't want to leave them behind where they can be used to kill other good people."

Michael obeyed quickly, picking up both Glocks. He found four extra magazines on the dead bodies and loaded them into the truck as well. Then he went to the state police cruiser. He searched the car and found a pump shotgun along with a box of double-aught shells. Then he opened up the trunk and saw the bodies of two state troopers.

"Colonel! I need you here!"

Buzz had been set up at the rear of the truck watching for danger. He ran up to the cruiser and looked into the trunk. He shook his head sadly.

"Michael, I want to bury them, but ... we don't have

time." And then he reconsidered. "But we can load them into the pick-up bed and give them a decent burial back in Hickory Flats."

It took five minutes for the two men to take the bodies out of the trunk and lift them up onto the tail gate of the truck. They rolled them both in and closed the gate.

Then Buzz went back to the trunk and pulled out the medical kit, which was a complete Basic Life Support Bag (BLS) bag. There was also an AED inside and he took that as well.

He turned to Michael. "Put these into the truck. I'm going to disable this cruiser, so it's not used on innocent people again. Buzz moved to the driver's seat and popped open the hood. He reached in with his knife and started cutting wires and slashing hoses. Then he walked around to each of the four tires and stabbed his knife into the side-walls.

The colonel took one final look around before rushing back over to the truck and jumping into the cab. Michael hopped in beside him. He took a quick look into the truck bed and put the truck in drive. He yelled back at Bob.

"Hold on tight, farm boy!"

And then he pulled away from the police cruiser and sped up as quickly as he safely could. Soon they were blowing through one stop sign after another at over 85 miles per hour.

He looked over at Michael. "Get on the CB radio and tell Cypress what our situation is. Our ETA is 20 minutes. We'll need boiling water, clean towels and a place to work on these two with lots of bright light. Tell him to fire up my generator."

Michael looked back at him at bit flustered. "He's 14 years old. I don't think he knows how to do that."

Buzz smiled slightly. "No, but your Uncle Johnny does."

Michael nodded and went to work.

K<small>AREN WAS WORKING IN THE KITCHEN WHEN</small> C<small>YPRESS</small> got the CB call. She'd been trying to keep busy while waiting for Mag and her boy to come home, knowing that she'd never get to sleep until they returned anyway. Cypress yelled out to her. "Mom! It's Michael. They're 20 minutes out!"

She ran into his bedroom where his comm gear was all set up and listened to Michael's voice. She thought to herself *Thank God he's still alive!* And then Michael's voice came over the radio.

"Dad's been shot in the shoulder. He'll survive if we can get him home in time to work on him. The colonel wants you to boil some water, get some towels ready and get a spot where we can work on him with lots of light. His house has the Generac, so Uncle Johnny can fire it up before we get there."

Karen reached over and took the microphone from her younger son. "Michael, are you okay?"

When he heard his mother's voice, Michael broke down and started to cry. He couldn't talk right away. Buzz reached across the cab and squeezed Michael's shoulder.

"Put it on hold, son!"

Michael nodded and quickly mastered his emotions. "Yeah, Mom. I'm just fine. Dad will be fine, too. But Abby is in bad shape. But we did find her."

A million thoughts ran through Karen's head, and she tried desperately to prioritize them and sort them out. Then she latched onto a sequence of tasks. She turned to Cypress.

"Go get your Uncle Johnny and tell him what's going on. He's out by the pole barn on watch. He needs to get to Buzzes' place and get the lights on and clear the kitchen table for your dad."

Cypress rushed out the door. And then she remembered what Michael had told her about his crush on Abby. "Don't worry about Abby, son. She's going to be okay. I'm going to drive over to the Vandenberg's and get Marie. She was a nurse for 20 years and worked in the emergency room. She'll know what to do."

Just then little Katy walked into the room, holding her dolly and rubbing sleep from her eyes. "What's wrong, Mommy?"

Karen set down the microphone and rushed over to her little girl. "Nothing, sweetheart. Daddy and Michael are on their way home is all. Mommy is talking to Michael."

That brought a tiny smile to her face. "Can I talk to Daddy?"

Karen quickly shook her head. "Not right now, honey. Daddy is tired from saving Abby and he's sleeping in the truck, but you can talk to him first thing in the morning. Go back to sleep now. Mommy will try and be more quiet."

She gave Katy a hug and sent her back into bed. Then she moved back to the microphone. "Is there anything else you need, Michael?"

Michael looked over at Buzz who shook his head in the negative. But Michael paused.

"Yeah, Mom. Please pray for us. We're not home yet, and we could use a little help from God."

Karen smiled sadly. "Roger that, son. I love you."

"I love you too, Mom."

And then she rushed out of the room and hopped into Bob Vandenberg's truck and drove like a lunatic all the way there.

TEN MINUTES LATER BUZZ NEARED THE CORNER OF Patterson and Chief Noonday Roads. Just as he cleared the hill, he saw four trucks parked in the middle of the intersection. There was a large, hand-painted sign up front that said "PAY TOLL". Buzz braked hard, sending Mag to the floor of the cab with a groan. He threw the truck in reverse and backed up to the north side of the rise where they could no longer see him. Michael already had his carbine up and at the ready.

Michael looked over at Buzz. "What do they mean by 'Pay Toll'?"

"That's a good question. One I can't answer."

Michael looked in the back onto the floor at his father. "Dad rolled off the seat. Should I put him back up again?"

Buzz shook his head. "Negative. He'll just fall back down again, especially if this toll booth thing goes south."

Bob Vandenberg leaned over the cab and spoke into the driver's-side window to Buzz. "Why are we stopping?"

A grim smile came over the colonel's face as he talked. "Oh, nothing we can't handle. Just Robbing Hood and a band of his merry men." While he talked, Buzz kept his eyes forward. "We got some highwaymen up ahead that want to charge a toll."

Bob shrugged. "How much?"

Michael responded. "We don't know. It's not on their sign."

"Then how do we know whether or not we can pay it?"

Buzz grunted out loud. "Exactly why we're not going to pay it. These guys are nothing but the country-bumpkin equivalent of the thugs who beat up your daughter. We let them get away with it and it'll encourage others to do the same. On the other hand, if we just kill them now, we don't have to worry about it anymore."

Bob looked down at his daughter lying in the back of

the truck. She was covered with a blanket, and her head was propped up on her pack.

"We can't just kill people because they're in our way. That's not right."

The colonel hopped out of the truck. He took the binoculars off the console and stepped forward just enough so he could see the intersection. He was up there for over a minute, then he stepped back again.

"Here's the situation. We've got four brand-new pick-up trucks, all with dealer plates. There are eight men that I can see, all armed with long guns. They've got lawn chairs set up with a campfire right in the middle of the road, and they're drinking beer."

Michael frowned, his teeth set firm. "I'm so sick of people taking advantage of the situation. Why can't people just be nice to each other?"

Buzz didn't answer. He just looked over at Bob. "What about you, farm boy?"

Bob didn't answer at first. He grabbed the optics out of the colonel's hand and moved to get a better view. While he was up there, a shot rang out, and he felt the bullet whiz by his head. Immediately, Bob dropped down to the pavement and crawled his way back to safety.

He stood up and brushed himself off, handing the binoculars back to the colonel. He looked into the back of the truck bed at his daughter, with her swollen and bloody face. And then he spoke softly through gritted teeth.

"On the other hand, maybe we should just kill them now."

Buzz smiled and called them back over to the truck. "Okay then. If we're going to be in a gunfight, we may as well win."

And then he stooped down to the shoulder over by the edge of the road and drew into the gravel with his finger.

"Here's how we're going to do this."

Fifteen minutes later everyone was in position. The colonel was the first to speak.

"Farm boy. Check in."

"I'm in position and ready."

"Michael Bravo. Check in."

"I'm in position, sir."

Buzz waited a few seconds, looking through the night vision goggles taking one last look before switching to the rifle scope. All three of the men had attached suppressors to their carbines for added stealth.

"Wait for my first shot. Then engage your assigned targets."

Buzz was located just northeast of the roadblock with a clear line of sight at the front and eastern trucks. He fired his first shot and then all hell broke loose. Within 10 seconds all the head lights were taken out. The men around the trucks scampered for cover, but now they were in darkness, except for the light of their campfire, unable to see what they were up against. Buzz watched through his scope as two men quickly threw water on the fire. The rifle fire ceased and soon, the roadblock was dark, except for the light of the moon.

Michael was hidden on the northwest corner of the roadblock, straight across the road from Buzz behind a walnut tree. Bob had remained back by the truck, lying in the prone position in the road. All three of them lined up shots, waiting for the signal. The colonel's voice boomed out from the darkness.

"Here's your situation, boys. We have you surrounded on all sides. We're in the dark, and we can shoot you anytime we want. If you don't want to die, I recommend you fire up those trucks you stole and beat feet outta here."

There was no answer. "You boys got one minute to leave before we open up."

Buzz waited the full minute then gave them an added 30 seconds. "Okay boys; time's up. You leaving or not?"

Buzz was 50 yards from the intersection, and he had seen the two men flank him to his left. He would deal with them in his own due time. Then a man's voice boomed into the night.

"We ain't leavin'! In fact, we aim on killin' y'all just fer fun. You ain't got nothin' but 22 rifles 'n we got AR-15s 'n M4s. We got full auto boy, 'n yer gonna die real fast."

The colonel shook his head sadly. *They think we have 22 rifles because our suppressors make our carbines sound smaller than they are. That's a costly mistake.*

And then all six of the men behind the trucks opened up on the colonel's position. He yelled through his microphone. "Engage! Engage!"

Michael took out one man immediately. Bob killed the leader who'd been talking. The colonel swung around to his left to deal with the oncoming threat, the two men who'd been trying to flank him. He moved to the other side of the tree to get better cover. And then he waited.

Michael shot one more and so did Bob. But the survivors were now hunkering down behind the engine block where they couldn't get off a clear shot at them. Michael started to belly crawl his way closer to the trucks.

The colonel's voice came over the comms. "I'm being flanked from south of my position. Michael Bravo, can you move around and get them from behind?"

"Roger that, colonel. I'm on my way."

Bob continued to watch from 100 yards away. He'd

never shot a man before, but he'd never needed to either. Right now he just knew that these men were standing between him and the safety of his daughter, and that's all he needed to know.

Michael was 30 yards away now, lying flat in the tall grass. He reached into his front cargo pants pocket and pulled out the M67 fragmentation grenade. He removed the safety clip and pulled the pin before throwing it from the prone position. The grenade hit the shoulder of the road and bounced several more feet along the pavement. The explosion was deafening, rocking the silence of the night, and pushing the lead pick-up truck over and into the closest truck. Just then Buzz came over the radio.

"You killed one more but the other one squeaked out the east side toward me. I got three hostiles now coming up from the south. Run straight toward the trucks and engage them from their left flank. Hurry! I'm about to be overrun!"

The first two hostiles were only 25 yards away now and headed straight toward the tree where Buzz was hiding. He fired from the prone position. One man dropped, but the other kept coming. He shot at the second, but missed. He was right on top of him now. Buzz scooted around to the west side of the tree to avoid the man's shots. They hadn't been lying. They did have full auto carbines. The bullets raked into the ground around him and the tree to his front.

Just then Michael reached the trucks and fired at the lead man. He missed twice but the third shot hit the man in the hip. He rolled over to one side and hit the ground hard. His M4 flew out of his hands and landed 10 feet away.

Then Michael saw the last man fleeing to the south. He propped his carbine up onto the hood of the southern-most truck and fired several times. The man kept running, and Michael let him go.

He heard the colonel in his earbud.

"All units report."

"Michael Bravo secure."

"Farm boy secure."

There was a short silence.

"Farm boy, bring down the transport."

"Roger that, colonel."

Michael put his night vision goggles back on and saw the colonel over to the northeast.

"Colonel, I'm coming your way."

"Roger that. Stay alert."

A few seconds later, they were both standing over the body of the man he'd shot in the hip. He was moaning his last.

Michael looked down at him and shook his head. "Why did they do this? You gave them every chance to do the right thing?"

The colonel reached over and put his arm on the boy's shoulder. "You're still a young soldier. But you have to understand that some people don't want to do the right thing. They're not like you and I. It's just not in them to do good, and when no one's there to stop them, then a lot of good people get hurt."

Michael knelt down beside the man and looked into his eyes. He saw the fear, but something else was lying deep down inside it. It was hatred.

Buzz barked out a command. "Get all their weapons and ammo. Then we roll!"

The man died, and they got back into their truck and drove away.

"*I'm a sheepdog. I live to protect the flock and confront the wolf. If you have no capacity for violence then you are a healthy productive citizen, a sheep. If you have a capacity for violence and no empathy for your fellow citizens, then you have defined an aggressive sociopath, a wolf. But what if you have a capacity for violence, and a deep love for your fellow citizens? What do you have then? A sheepdog, a warrior, someone who is walking the hero's path. Someone who can walk into the heart of darkness, into the universal human phobia, and walk out unscathed.*"

—*LTC(RET) Dave Grossman, RANGER, Ph.D., author of "On Killing."*—

KILLOLOGY

Lieutenant Colonel Dave Grossman, a retired Army Ranger, is the world's foremost expert on the topic of killology. While I was interviewing Dave for *Frontlines of Freedom* radio a few months back, I asked the colonel "exactly what is killology?" Dave told me "Killology is the study of the legal use of deadly force; it is the legal taking of another human life." He went on to tell me there's been tons of research done on serial killers, lunatics, etc. For some strange reason people are enamored with murderers; they want to know how they tick; why they kill; what caused them to deviate from the rest of the human race.

Frankly, I agree with Colonel Grossman when he says, and I paraphrase, "It's more important to know how to defend against the killers, than it is to know why they do what they do." People have been trying to figure out insanity and mental illness for centuries with little progress. I doubt, even in our current state of hubris, we'll be able to succeed where others have failed. Let's be blunt here. I'm not that smart, however, I am smart enough to know that one good way to stop a bad guy with a gun is to kill him or throw him in prison for the rest of his life. I have very little faith in the criminal justice system, and rehabilitation is a rarity. It has long been known that a small minority of the human race perpetrates a large majority of the violent crime.

Colonel Grossman calls these violent criminals "wolves," and the wolves usually continue to prey upon the sheep with impunity until someone stops them, many times with the aid of deadly force.

Skip Coryell,
Civilian Combat: the Concealed Carry Book

"So they set out and went from village to village, proclaiming the good news and healing people everywhere."

Luke 9:6 (NIV)

CHAPTER 16

The House that Buzz Built

BY THE TIME THEY REACHED THE colonel's house, it was lit up like a Christmas tree. Karen was waiting at the front door with her carbine on a one-point sling. She ran to the truck as soon as it slid to a stop.

"Where is he?"

Michael hopped out and opened the back door of the truck. She rushed in and looked at Mag's face in the dim illumination of the cab's overhead light. Karen peered down into his blood-covered face and grit her teeth. She screamed at him without even realizing it.

"Don't you die, Michael Magnum Jacobs! If you die I will never forgive you!"

Mag's eyes fluttered and then remained open. He saw the blurred image of her face, hovering above him, like a beautiful angel on methamphetamines.

He smiled. "Sorry I'm late, honey. Traffic was pretty rough."

She heard his voice and broke down crying. Michael gently pushed past her. "Mom, we need to get him inside. Is Mrs. Vandenberg here yet?"

Karen seemed confused for a few seconds, then she answered. "Ah, yes. She's in the dining room. The table is set up and ready."

Buzz came around and spoke to Bob. "Bob, just keep your daughter comfortable. We'll be back for her in a minute." He and Michael carefully pulled Mag out of the back seat and carried him inside through the front door and into the dining room. Mag groaned every time they took a step. The colonel was as sympathetic as his personality would allow. "Shut up, Marine. Suck it up!"

They laid him carefully on the table. There were four light bulbs in the fixture above. Marie had replaced the 60-watt bulbs with 100-watt, and the room was very bright. She moved quickly over Mag's chest before barking out orders. "Get all this equipment off him. I need a bare chest in 30 seconds."

Michael and Buzz removed his tactical vest and his body armor, and then Buzz pulled out a knife and cut off his shirt. "Stay still, Marine. I don't want to cut you any more than you already are."

They quickly finished and stepped back so Marie could move closer. "Mag, can you hear me?"

Mag's eyes fluttered open in the bright light. He opened his mouth to speak, but the words came out soft and slight. "Can I get some more apple pie?"

Marie smiled and nodded assurance to Karen. Karen pushed forward and bent down to kiss her husband on the forehead. When she moved away there was blood on her lips, but she didn't seem to notice the salty taste.

Then Marie turned to Karen. "Honey, will you please go out and help get my daughter in here?"

Karen nodded and then turned to her son. "Michael, will you help me, please." They both exited the room, leaving Buzz and Marie there with Mag.

She leaned down and took a closer look at the wound. "Tell me what happened, Buzz."

Buzz shrugged. "We walked into an ambush. He got shot. I'm guessing you'll find a handgun round somewhere inside the right side of his chest."

Marie nodded. She had a large bowl filled with alcohol atop the table. She dipper her hands down into it and scrubbed. Then she probed the wound with her fingers.

"Yes, I agree. If it was a rifle round, he'd be dead already. He's still conscious, but in stage two shock from blood loss."

Buzz hovered close by like a mother hen assessing a possible threat. When he felt reassured that Marie knew what she was doing, he backed away a step.

"Don't go anywhere, colonel. I may need an extra pair of hands to hold him down while I'm digging inside for the bullet. But first things first. We need to get some saline inside him and get him stable."

Buzz nodded. "Do you have saline?"

Marie shook her head. "No, but I can make some here in the kitchen, then we can rig up a home-made IV."

Buzz glanced over at the counter top to his left and saw the array of plastic tubing, clamps and a 2-liter Mountain Dew bottle.

"I've already gotten a head start on it."

Buzz smiled softly. "Let me help you out with that. Just wait here. I'll be back in two minutes"

Marie looked on confused as he walked away, but she continued treating her patient nonetheless.

"Are you still with me, Mag?"

"Yep. Still here."

"You feeling dizzy or weak right now?"

She grabbed his arm and took his pulse again.

"Yeah, a bit, but not like it was."

She smiled reassuringly.

"Well, your pulse is stable now, a bit elevated, but that should calm down when we get more fluid inside you. Looks like the bullet glanced off your armor and into your chest at an angle and that's what saved you. No major blood vessels severed, missed the lung and the clavicle."

And then Marie surprised him by saying,"I think you're just being a big baby about all this."

Mag's body hurt all over, but this unexpected bout of humor coming from a medical expert made him laugh. He immediately regretted it as more pain surged through his chest.

"Yes, you're right, but don't tell Karen. I plan on milking this wound for all the sympathy I can get."

Marie laughed as well. "Can't say as I blame you. Best to get what you can out of a bad situation." And then she changed the subject. "Is this where that robber stabbed you a few weeks back?"

Mag nodded but said nothing. "Well, you'll be happy to know that it's healing nicely." "

Just then the colonel stepped back into the room. He was carrying an olive-drab chest made of heavy plastic. He set it on the floor beside Marie.

"Anything you can use in here?"

Marie bent down and opened the latches. She caught her breath when she saw the array of medical gear inside.

Right on top was a TSSI M9 Medical Bag in digital camo.

"Where did you get this?"

Buzz smiled, stifling a laugh. "It was a gift. Let's just call it part of my severance package and leave it at that."

Marie pulled out the medical bag and placed it on the table beside Mag. She opened the main compartment and was pleased to see exactly what she needed.

She opened one of the inner pouches and pulled out an IV kit, some plastic tubing as well as a bag of 0.9 percent sodium chloride solution.

Marie quickly went to work and with the colonel's help had the IV up and running into Mag's arm in just a few minutes.

"How are you doing, Mag?"

Mag tried to laugh it off again, but coughed a bit before regaining his composure.

"Can you put some coffee in that IV? I think that would help me out."

Marie smiled again. She'd always liked Mag's cheerful disposition. He was going to need it before she was done with him tonight.

"Not right now, Mag. Perhaps in the morning." Then she pulled the stethoscope and blood pressure monitor out of the M9 bag and checked his vital signs.

Mag looked up. His eyes were adjusted to the light now. "Am I going to make it?"

The colonel scoffed at him. "You Marines are supposed to be so tough, but I'm just not seeing it."

Mag ignored his remark.

"Colonel, help me roll him to his side so I can take a look."

Buzz helped her and a concerned look came over the nurse's face, as she confirmed there was no exit wound.

They rolled him back so he was facing up again.

"Mag, I've got good news and bad news."

Mag's eyes squinted in the bright light. "Okay, give me the bad news first."

Marie paused. "The bullet is still inside you, and it has to come out."

Mag let that thought sink in. "Okay, so what's the good news?"

Marie smiled just a little. "The good news is I'm not going to let the colonel take it out."

Mag switched his gaze over to Buzz, who was grinning from ear to ear. "That's good news, Marie." And then he added. "Good call. I have total confidence in you."

But the colonel was quick to respond. "You should let me do it, doc. I can make it fast and painless for him. We won't even need anesthetic."

Marie frowned. "Well, that's the other bad news. We don't have any anesthetic."

Mag started to open his mouth to say something, but then quickly shut it again. Marie turned to her left and picked up a thick, hard-covered book off the table. It was a medical book. She searched through the index until she found what she was looking for.

"Ah, hear it is. How to perform a frontal lobotomy."

Mag's eyes widened in terror. The colonel roared with laughter. Marie reached over and gently stroked his forehead. "It's okay, Mag. Just kidding."

She started to read to herself. "Oh my. This is going to hurt." And then she looked down at him. "Are you sure you can handle this, Mag?"

Mag looked over at the colonel and grit his teeth defiantly. He saw the incessant smile, gloating down on him. He refused to give the colonel the satisfaction of seeing him suffer. And when he responded, it was with all the tough, Marine Corps confidence he could muster.

"Bring it on doc! I was born to handle this."

She smiled and nodded.

Out in the back of the truck, Karen and Bob knelt beside Abby. She was conscious now, but her voice was quiet and barely discernible.

"Hi Daddy."

Bob reached his head down and kissed his daughter on the swollen cheek. He tried to keep from crying.

"Hello, sweetheart."

"Where am I?"

"We just got you back to the Jacobs house."

"Where's Mom?"

He narrowed his eyes as he spoke. "She's in there working on Mr. Jacobs. He got shot, but he's going to be okay."

Abby had a hundred questions, but was too weak to ask them. The cab light was on, and she could see Michael standing in the background.

"Hello, Michael."

Michael knelt down in the truck bed, littered with military gear and the bodies of the two dead state troopers.

"Hi Abby. Good to see you again. It's been a while."

He didn't know what to say, and there was a clumsy silence. Finally, Karen took control.

"Boys, we need to get Abby inside and in bed where she can be more comfortable. There are some things obstructing the tail gate. Will you clear the way, please?"

Michael looked back over at his mother and nodded. He and Bob hopped out of the bed and opened the tailgate. They then carefully picked up the fallen troopers

and carefully laid them, one at a time, on the ground beside the truck. They would have to wait until tomorrow
for burial. They moved some other gear and then they
were ready.

As carefully as they could, the three of them slid Abby
to the tail gate and then picked her up. Michael got her
legs, Karen her middle, and her father held up by her head.

Just then they heard a loud scream from inside the
house and then another and another.

Karen looked down at Abby in the moonlight. "It's
okay, little one. It's just my husband. He can take it."

Abby closed her eyes. Suddenly her head hurt and
was throbbing too much to bear. She fell asleep again.
The three took her inside and set her on the bed in the
guest room. Karen covered her up as gently as she could.
Then she went to the bathroom and came back with a wet
wash cloth and a bowl of warm water. As Abby's weeping
father looked on, Karen cleaned her wounds as best she
could. Eventually Mag's screams faded, got quieter and
then went away altogether.

"Stay with her, Bob. I'm going to check on Mag."

MICHAEL WAS LOOKING DOWN AT HIS DAD, HOLD-
ing his right hand. Karen was on the other side holding his
left. Buzz was no longer needed and had retreated to his
command center in the basement to monitor radio broadcasts. Mag was asleep now, totally exhausted. Marie had
removed the bullet. It was a nine millimeter semi-jacketed
hollow point. It was on the table now, coated in Mag's
blood. It had misshaped upon impact with the body armor which had lessened the penetration, thereby making
it easier for Marie to find it and dig it out.

"Your husband's a lucky man, Karen. He could have

died from blood loss, but all the vital organs and blood vessels were missed."

Karen looked up with tears in her eyes. "Thanks so much, Marie. You saved his life."

Marie smiled. "Well, not until he got shot trying to rescue my daughter. He's a good man."

There was a silence. Karen reached up and brushed the light, brown hair away from her husband's eyes. "Yes, I know." She paused. "He's the best a woman could hope for."

Marie gave her a hug and then left the room to seek out her daughter. Karen looked over to her son on the other side of the table.

"Are you okay, son?"

Michael tried to toughen up, but this time it didn't work. His tears flowed down his cheeks. "I don't want to be a soldier anymore, Mom."

Karen laid Mag's hand gently down and walked around the table to comfort her son. She wrapped her arms around him and he buried his head onto her shoulder. She shushed his crying. "It's okay. Michael. Rest now. You did your job, and I'm very proud of you."

Michael cried in his mother's arms for several minutes. Finally, he stood up, retrieved his carbine and headed toward the door. He called over his shoulder.

"I'll get Cypress into bed and check on Katy while you watch over Dad. Then I'll be on watch the rest of the night. Don't worry about them."

Karen watched him leave, and then bent back down to her husband. She wouldn't worry now, all the men she loved were safely home.

TSSI M9 MEDICAL BAG

The M9 Medical Bag was designed by a Special Forces Medic while he was on duty in Afghanistan. He was dissatisfied with the medical bag he was issued by the Army, so he came up with one of his own that was better organized. The M9 is a complete medical bag designed to keep the injured person alive during what's called "The Golden Hour."

gold·en hour
nounMEDICINE
the first hour after the occurrence of a traumatic injury, considered the most critical for successful emergency treatment.

Oxford Dictionary

The M9 has everything needed to stop bleeding and start breathing.

TSSI M9 MEDICAL BAG CONTENTS

- Petzl Headlamp with Multi-Color Lighting
- TACOPS™ Tactical Rescue Knife
- QuikClot® Z-fold Combat Gauze Packs
- SOFTT-W Tourniquets
- Chest Seal
- Compression Bandages
- Emergency Bandage, 4"
- Compressed Gauze Packs
- Burn Dressing, 18"x 18" (Sterile)
- Nasopharyngeal Airways

Contents (Continued)

- Surgical Lubricant Foil Packs
- Oral Airway, 80mm
- Oral Airway, 100mm
- Pocket Bag Valve Mask
- Disposable Suction Device
- Elastic Bandages, 4"x 5yds
- SAM® Splints, 36"
- Gauze Pads, 4"x 4" (Sterile)
- Gauze Pads, 2"x 2' (Sterile)
- Adhesive tape, 1"x 10yds
- Triangular Bandages, 40"x 40"
- Trauma Shears
- Straight Kelly Hemostat, 6.25"
- Mosquito Hemostats, 3.5"
- Fine Point Forceps, 4.5"
- Adhesive Bandages, 7/8"x 3"
- Fingertip Adhesive Bandages
- Knuckle Adhesive Bandages
- Alcohol Prep Pads
- Iodine Prep Pads
- Nitrile Gloves
- Permanent felt-tip marker, Blue
- TacNotes 4'x6"

For more information go to tssi-ops.com.

> *"Then your light will break forth like the dawn, and your healing will quickly appear; then your righteousness will go before you, and the glory of the Lord will be your rear guard."*
>
> *Isaiah 58:8 (NIV)*

CHAPTER 17

The Jacobs Home - The Next Day

WHEN **M**AG WOKE UP THE NEXT day, he was pleased to feel the smooth, soft cotton sheets against his skin. He opened his eyes and looked up at his bedroom ceiling, recognizing the familiar fly specks and smudges that he'd woken up to every day since he and Karen had moved into this house. And he thought to himself *Thank God! It was all a bad dream!* And then he tried to roll over to go back to sleep and surging pain roared through the right half of his body from the bullet wound.

No, it was not a dream. And then he remembered it all. The Chinese had seeded America with a deadly pandemic, killing 90 percent of the population. Then the shooting war had started. American cities were now radioactive piles of rubble. Anarchy was loosed upon the world, and it truly was the end of the world as we know it.

Mag laid there in bed for a few moments, waiting for the pain to slowly subside, so he could get out of bed and get some work done. He remembered the night before, the shoot-out at Cornerstone University, the explosions, the bullets ripping into walls and ceilings all around him. He remembered the colonel laying down cover fire, and then shoving gauze into the hole in his shoulder. There was a fondness when he recalled how his son had carried him out of the violent maelstrom and into safety.

He thought about Michael now. He was a good kid, and he wondered what effect all this violence was having on him. Mag sighed. He used to worry about the boys playing violent video games, or watching violent movies, but now ... the violence was no longer make-believe. It was as real as the rain pattering against his bedroom window.

Mag looked at the rain hitting the glass now; it had a distinct sound, and a calming effect on him that seemed to soothe and relax him like a healing balm, like an ointment for his heart that returned his focus back to God. And then he asked God *why*, in the quiet of his heart. *Why did I get shot, God? Why was Abby beaten? Why don't I have any electricity? Why did you wait until my book sales finally started to increase before ending the world. I was on the cusp of literary success, and now ...* it was all gone.

God rarely answered Mag's questions, certainly not audibly at least. Just then the door opened a crack and a tiny head peeked in. Mag saw one eye of his daughter, and then the door opened a little more. Katy's face appeared and then she walked in upon seeing that Mag was awake. She ran toward the bed, and Mag braced for her jump onto his body and the racking pain that would follow, but at the last second she stopped and stood by the bed.

"Hello, Daddy. How is your bullet hole feeling?"

Mag smiled weakly. He looked over at his little caboose, and all the negative feelings of "why" seemed to melt away, at least for now.

"It hurts, Katy."

She nodded. "Mommy says I can't jump on you today. So I hope it's better by tomorrow. Can I see your bullet hole? I never saw one before."

Mag's smile grew a little wider. He was so proud of his little girl. "Let's talk to Mommy about that, honey. Daddy hasn't even seen it yet. It might be pretty ugly."

She shrugged and moved a bit closer. "I spose so." Then she rested her hands on the covers for a moment before reaching up to stroke his face. Her tiny hands were soft and gentle and filled with love. Mag closed his eyes and fought back a tear. *He'd almost died and left his little girl behind.* He started to chastise himself for feeling sorry for himself and questioning God. He needed to be more positive, to pass on hope and love to his children, especially now during the apocalypse. Their world was filled with danger and violence and evil and fear. But God had the antithesis of all that, and it was Mag's job to show Katy and Michael, Cypress and even his wife Karen, how to live life to the full, to show them that life was worth living, that indeed God had a purpose for their family. Suddenly, he felt ashamed of his weakness. They needed him, and they needed him to be strong.

Mag was reminded of the story of queen Esther and the phrase "And who knows but that you have come to your royal position for such a time as this?"

Katy stopped caressing his cheek. "You need a shave, Daddy." And then she ran out of the room.

Mag thought to himself, the world has been destroyed.

Then he scratched that thought out of his mind. No, not destroyed, but remade. God has pushed the reset button, and now all the things that were most important before are once again paramount and undeniable.

"I am a child of God. I was created to praise Him." Mag closed his eyes and begged God's forgiveness for his lack of faith. The world was shattered and shaken, but God had placed them all on the ark and spared their lives. They were alive. They had survived the apocalypse.

Katy ran back into the room. She was holding his electric shaver. Little Mary walked in behind her slowly and shyly. She stood behind Katy at the side of the bed, holding her favorite doll.

"Mom charged it on the solar-powered battery pack. She knew you were going to need it." Katy turned on the button and the charger started to hum. Then she turned to Mary and spoke as if Mag wasn't even there.

"Now here's how you do it. And don't press too hard or you might rip his face off."

She moved the razor gently back and forth across his cheek, pressing just hard enough to remove the stubble. And then she turned back to Mary. "See? You try it now."

Little Mary stepped forward slowly and grasped the electric razor in her right hand. She pressed down hard and drug it across Mag's cheek. He fought back the wince as the blades bit into his skin, but he said nothing. Mary did the right cheek, then Katy did the left. They traded off and on for his throat and then his upper lip and even his nose.

"You see, Mary. I'm gonna share my Daddy with you, so you have to know how to take care of him. And if you're good, he'll show us the bullet hole in his shoulder."

And Mag suddenly put things into perspective. *Yes,*

life was rough, but they were still alive. Mary had lost both her parents, but his family was still intact. Others had been brutally killed at the hands of criminals like the ones in Grand Rapids, and even some of his friends had been murdered right here in Hickory Flats.

Millions had been incinerated by nuclear explosion or been slowly cooked by radiation from the inside out. But his family was alive. Most had died slowly over two days of intense agony as the corona virus had destroyed their bodies. He tried to raised his right arm and stroked first Katy's cheek and then Mary's. Katy smiled and put her arm around Mary. And then it occurred to Mag; *they were healing each other.* He smiled.

"Katy, will you please tell your mother that I need to speak with her?"

Katy quickly reached over and pecked Mag on the cheek. Then she turned to Mary. "Go ahead. I'm sharing."

Mary moved forward slowly, encouraged by Katy until she gently kissed him on the cheek. "See? I told you he was a good Daddy!"

And then she turned to run out of the room, calling over her shoulder. "C'mon! Let's charge this thing up so we can do it again!"

And then they were gone and Mag was alone once more. He looked out the window and watched the rain hit the glass, then gently slide down the pane in tiny rivers.

Just then Karen walked into the room. "Good morning, sunshine!"

Mag smiled and held his good arm out to her. She came forward and sat on the bed beside him. He winced a bit in the pain, but grit his teeth to hold it back.

"How bad is the pain?"

Mag smiled. "Not too bad. It only hurts when I

breathe."

Karen reached over and gently stroked his clean-shaven cheek. "Well, you should've stayed home like I wanted you to. If you hadn't left then you wouldn't be lying in that bed all shot up right now."

Mag knew that she was half joking, but still mad at him for endangering his life. He thought about how to best say his next words, but couldn't devise a better way to say it, so he just blurted it out. "Abby would be dead right now if we hadn't gone."

Karen reached up to twirl her hair with her finger, the way she always did when she was under stress. Mag waited.

"I know that, Mag. I'm not saying you did the wrong thing. I'm saying I love you and I was worried sick about you while you were gone." Tears came to her eyes. She looked away at the rain on the window and then quickly back again. "If you died I don't think I could handle it." And then she added. "I get my strength from you."

Mag nodded and grabbed her hand in his own, softly caressing it the same way Katy had touched his own cheek. "A cord of three strands is not easily broken."

She looked at Mag quizzically. "Three strands?"

He smiled up at her. "Of course. You, me and the Lord."

Karen smiled and then nodded in agreement. "Ya know what I like about you?"

Mag laughed. "Everything?"

She laughed too. "No. Not everything. But ... you are strong where I'm weak. You keep your faith when I doubt. You stay positive when I'm filled with turmoil."

Mag thought about that for a second. If only she knew about his own doubts and his own fears, how he had temporarily lost his own faith just a few minutes ago in this very bed. But ... he kept that to himself.

"Well, part of that is your own doing, sweetheart." He looked over at the rain as he talked. "I don't want to let you and the kids down. I don't want to ever do anything that might bring shame upon this family. I want you proud of me, so I fight to be the best person I can for you."

Karen let him finish before she broke down and sobbed against his chest. Mag ignored the pain as her head bobbed up and down on his sternum.

"I love you so much, Mag."

Mag smiled and added.

"Yes, honey, but I loved you first."

And then he cried along with her.

Epilogue - 1 week later

MICHAEL PULLED INTO THE DRIVEWAY AND ROLLED to a stop on the gravel. He got out of the truck and pushed his carbine onto his back out of the way. Then he grabbed the pack and walked past the pole barn and up to the side porch. Once there, he knocked on the door. A few seconds later, Marie Vandenberg opened the door to him. She had a Beretta M9 pistol in a drop-leg holster, courtesy of the colonel. Michael nodded before addressing her.

"Good evening Mrs. Vandenberg."

She smiled and relaxed when she saw it was Michael. "Come on in, Michael. Would you like some pie?"

Michael smiled. "Is that a trick question?"

He walked inside and followed her to the kitchen. He set the pack down on the large, dining room table.

"The colonel asked me to bring you this extra Medical pack. He wants you to have it."

Marie looked over at the bag and smiled warmly. "That colonel is gruff, but he's a good man inside."

Michael nodded his agreement. "He's kind of like a grizzly bear with chocolate cream filling inside."

Marie laughed out loud as she cut him a slice of pie and placed it on the table in front of him. Michael looked at it and his mouth began to water.

"Thank you, Ma'am." He quickly bowed his head and thanked God silently for the food. He took a small bite and savored it in his mouth. He chewed, swallowed and then spoke again. "I want to thank you for helping my dad."

"So how is my patient doing today?"

Michael laughed. "Great! Mom had all she could do to keep him in bed today. But she won like she usually does."

Marie nodded her understanding. "Funny how that happens, Michael. Your mother is a very good woman. I'm sure she'll have him up and around in no time. His wounds will heal, barring any last-minute infection."

"Well, we are all mighty grateful to you."

She waved him off. "Don't be silly, Michael. It's I who should be thanking you. You saved my daughter's life, and I'll never forget that."

Suddenly, Michael felt a bit clumsy with his emotions. "So, how is she, Abby I mean? Is she okay now?"

Marie smiled. "Thanks for asking. Physically she'll be okay. But it's going to take a lot of time to heal inside. She's still adjusting to what happened to her and what she had to do."

Michael closed his eyes briefly and nodded. "I understand that. I'm dealing with the same kind of thing."

And then he looked up from the pie. "Do you think,

perhaps ... that I could talk to her? I may be able to cheer her up a bit."

Marie thought about it for a time. Then she nodded. "Follow me."

They went into the living room and Abby was in the recliner asleep. Marie whispered in his ear. "Just sit here until she wakes up. I have work to do."

Michael hesitated for just a moment. Then he nodded and sat down in a smaller chair across from Abby. Marie left and he watched Abby sleep. He watched as her chest rose and fell with the rhythm of her breathing. A few minutes later, her eyelids fluttered and then she opened them.

Michael didn't know what to say, so he remained quiet. These days he was better at fighting than expressing tender emotions. Abby was the first to speak. "You saved me."

Michael nodded. "Well, I was in the neighborhood, and it was the least I could do."

He added. "You look better. How are you feeling?"

She smiled apprehensively. "Better. The swelling and pain is down. Mom says I have a concussion but no lasting damage."

Michael shifted nervously in his seat. "And how are you feeling inside?"

That question caught her off guard. She thought about it for several seconds before deciding whether or not to answer it.

"I feel broken and torn, in a lot of different ways. How about you?"

Michael made eye contact with her. She had beautiful blue eyes and long, blonde hair. "I feel damaged and scarred, but ... I think I'm healing up okay."

And then she asked him. "How old are you, Michael?"

He answered right away. "I'll be 17 in two months. How old are you?"

She smiled. "I'm 19." And then she looked him up and down carefully. "How tall are you, Michael?"

"I'm six-one."

"Hmmm, I wonder why I never noticed you before."

But Abby had noticed him now. He was young, strong, polite, confident and secure. And ... he was handsome. She felt something strange inside that surprised her, but she pushed it back inside.

"Do you think there are other kids out there like us, Michael?"

He shrugged. "Maybe. I don't know how many or how far away they are, but I know there are others out there. Not all of them are good though."

She frowned. "Yes, I agree."

And then they talked together for over two hours, about everything. About the old days, the new days, the family and the apocalypse. But, most of all, they talked about their feelings.

Unknown to them, Marie Vandenberg listened from the kitchen as she cooked dinner. And she nodded her head with approval.

Here ends book 2 of *The Covid Chronicles*, but there are many more challenges to face and more dangers to overcome for Mag and his family in this new apocalyptic world. Thank you so much for reading my story.

Please do me a favor now and write a positive review and put it on Amazon. That really does help with sales. Also, please tell your friends about the book via social networking.

And now, I'll get busy writing book 3 in the series. It's coming soon!

Skip Coryell lives with his wife and children in Michigan. He works full time as a professional writer, and *The Covid Chronicles, Surviving the Apocalypse* is his 16th published book. He is an avid hunter and sportsman, a Marine Corps veteran, and a graduate of Cornerstone University. You can listen to Skip as he co-hosts the syndicated military talk radio show *Frontlines of Freedom* on frontlinesoffreedom.com. You can also hear his weekly podcast *The Home Defense Show* at homedefenseshow. com

For more details on Skip Coryell, or to contact him personally, go to his website at skipcoryell.com

Complete God Virus series!

Skip Coryell

This is 4 books in one! The complete 4-book God Virus apocalyptic adventure series beneath one cover. Suddenly, the lights went out, not just in one town or village, but all across the world. It was an act of cyber terrorism that plunged the world into the heart of darkness, into the 1000-year night, letting loose the demons of a billion souls, pitting dark against light, causing each person everywhere to choose sides. Not since Stephen King's "The Stand" has there been an apocalyptic thriller of such epic proportions. Read the entire 4-book series and see what happens when society's thin veneer of civility is stripped away. "The God Virus" series is gripping, seething and oozing with the best and worst humanity has to offer.

I started carrying a pistol almost 20 years ago, and I've been a member of a church safety team for about 15 years now. The church safety team is like other ministries in that we are serving the body of Christ, but there is one very distinct and important difference. It might get you killed.

I've been a Sunday school teacher, even Sunday School Superintendent. I've served on musical teams. I've been an usher. I've even helped in the children's ministry where they expected me to dance up and down to silly songs while making ridiculous hand motions. (Thank God there are no existing pictures for that one. It wasn't pretty.)

However, none of those jobs ever required me to take a bullet for the flock. As a Sunday School teacher, I was never expected to run towards gunshots while drawing my firearm. Most Sunday School teachers don't carry pepper spray; they don't practice open-handed skills to become proficient at taking a man to the ground and putting him in zip ties. They are not trained in the subtle arts of interrogation and visually identifying physical threats, like who is armed and who is not.

It's a different kind of ministry, requiring a different kind of Christian. However, all these concerns are not restricted to the church safety team, because they apply to any Christian who decides to carry a gun.

If you are considering carrying a gun or joining a church safety team, then, this book is a must-listen for you. You should not go into the job lightly, as there are many things to consider. Can you take a human life? Killing a fellow human being is not and should not be a natural and easy thing to do. It should be tough. It may take years of prayer and study and self-reflection before you decide the answer. Do you want to carry a gun? It's a nuisance, a total life change, and a bona fide pain in the butt. Carrying a gun dictates every facet of your life: how you treat others, what you wear, how you talk, and how you walk. It's not for everyone.

Are you willing to die to protect the ones you love? How about strangers? Will you die to protect someone you haven't even met yet. Are you willing to spend lots of time and money on training and equipment? Less than one percent of the concealed carry population ever go on to take training that is not required by the government. That statistic should scare you.

Buying a gun doesn't make you a gun fighter any more than buying a guitar makes you a rock star. We are called by God to excellence in everything we do. The gun is a powerful tool. The sacrifice you make could be supreme. It is a life-or-death decision. This book was written to empower and encourage Christians who decide to carry concealed. You are an elite corps of individuals. You are warriors. Welcome to the club! - Skip Coryell

If masculinity is toxic, then Jack Ruger is the cultural equivalent of a raging bull on steroids. Born and raised in the cold and frozen northern paradise of Michigan's upper peninsula, Chief of Police Jack Ruger is sworn to protect and defend the citizens of Jackpine. So when escaped killer Bobby Lee Harper descends on the town, threatening to kill him and all he holds dear, it's a formal declaration of war, and only one man will survive.

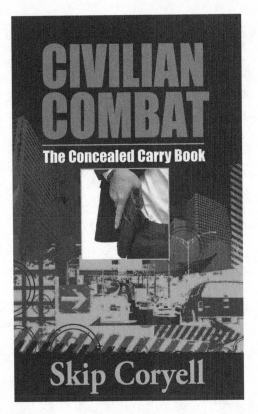

More and more people across the country are seeing the dangers in society and deciding to carry concealed to protect themselves and their families. Skip's book lays it out step by step, teaching you how to protect and defend the ones you love. Read his book and get the benefit of his 19 years of teaching experience and his lifetime of training for this important role in society. *Civilian Combat* is also a great teaching tool for other concealed carry instructors as well. It's a complete curriculum with a final test as well as important points to remember and a list of excellent resources in your journey to personal and family protection.

THE HOME DEFENSE SHOW

Skip is the creator and host of *The Home Defense Show*, a weekly 1-hour podcast about all things home, family and personal defense.

The Home Defense Show podcast is now available on iTunes, Google Play, Spreaker and Sticher. You can also find it on my YouTube channel. This should make it easier than ever for you to listen to my sweet angelic voice coming to you from deep inside the bowels of a great big empty. Don't forget to subscribe.

For more info go to homedefenseshow.com

FRONTLINES OF FREEDOM RADIO

You can hear authors Denny Gillem and Skip Coryell on one of your local stations on the number 1 military talk show in America. *Frontlines of Freedom* is syndicated on over 180 stations, and is also available as a podcast on frontlinesoffreedom.com.

Books by Skip Coryell

We Hold These Truths
Bond of Unseen Blood
Church and State
Blood in the Streets
Laughter and Tears
RKBA: Defending the Right to Keep and Bear Arms
Stalking Natalie
The God Virus
The Shadow Militia
The Saracen Tide
The Blind Man's Rage
Civilian Combat - The Concealed Carry Book
Concealed Carry for Christians
Jackpine Strong
The Covid Chronicles: Surviving the Upgrade
The Covid Chronicles: Surviving the Apocalypse